The Forgotten Mermaid

By Gregga J. Johnn

The Forgotten Mermaid by Gregga J. Johnn

Copyright © 2015 Gregga J. Johnn & Story-in-the-Wings. All rights reserved.

No part of this book may be reproduced or transmitted in any form or by any means, graphic, electronic, or mechanical, including photocopying, recording, taping, or by any information storage retrieval system, without the permission, in writing, of the publisher.

For more information, send a letter to:

Email: greggajjohnn@gmail.com

Story-in-the-Wings at Springhill Farm

1446 Arrowhead Rd

Cedar Rapids, Ia. 52314

For information about special discounts for bulk purchases, please contact Gregga J. Johnn, at

greggajjohnn@gmail.com

ISBN: 978-1517159016

One

Four hundred years ago, when the high seas were still full of raw adventure, there was a moving island. Held in the prison of the island's solitude was a forgotten mermaid. She was not forgotten because none remembered where she was, or even who she was. Nay. She was in prison on purpose and for good reason. It was *she* who had forgotten herself.

No longer did the fish woman remember the delight of her mermaid magic. For hardship of the heart had tethered darkness and entwined numbness against her soul, transforming her into a siren: a beast of gorgeous terror and enchanting madness. Those who answered or pursued her calling now, suffered greatly in her demise.

Luminescent shimmers from the worm droppings gave a soft, blue glow to slimy cave walls. The water plashed in careless rhythm as the sucking and slurping sounds that dripped from her blood soaked mouth echoed in an eerie chorus.

The siren feasted, again.

Her tail draped casually along and down the rocky outcropping and the end fins wavered back and forth in time with the moving tide. She sighed, almost bored, as her razor teeth tore into his biceps. She chewed somberly.

The Forgotten Mermaid   by Gregga J. Johnn

In her mind, she wandered memory halls, keeping distance in check to ensure no real emotion touched her frozen heart. She was just too tired to cry, too tired to scream, and for now, too tired to even sing anymore. Perhaps the freshness of his meat might restore her interest. She doubted it, sniffing distractedly and wiping her nose with the back of her wrist. He tasted good. That was at least something.

She sucked a random string of skin out of her silvery teeth with a blackened tongue and took another bite. She chewed and swallowed then sighed. And the glow worms continued to shimmer about her disgusting beauty.

Far away, cutting through a bustling filth-cracked port town, a grungy sailor, by name of Brice, pulled the greasy rag around his neck over his nose and closed up his wool collar against the biting wind.

Frost came quickly on the ocean's edge. But this year it seemed that with each crashing wave, the foaming ice would break off and slice into the very air, tearing into the throats of all who dared to breathe.

Brice crunched water shards under boot and pushed up the stone steps from the lower quay, up to the town streets. A blast of stench assaulted his nostrils even behind his linen mask and he bent his Captain's hat against the grime in the air.

Captain's hat, indeed. He snorted in disgust at his own misfortune and misgivings. What good was a Captain if none would follow him?

Yet, still he continued dogging his way on his path. His path; predetermined by a miracle that changed his life forever when he was but a small boy, was the path that poured derision and ridicule on him as his infamy grew with each new docking at each new port town. He wondered if his fame preceded him here. He would know soon enough.

Passing an open fire pit that was frosted with spitting hordes of rank sailors, Captain Brice saw the drunken nudging and snickering out of the corner of his eye. He counted off the seconds until he heard,

"Oi! Cap't Delusion, you found your tail of love, yet?" the frothy fire warmers took swigs of their sloshing brews, laughed in a loud chorus, and snorted at the lone dreamer.

Apparently news of his quest to prove the existence of mermaids had indeed arrived before him. That would certainly make finding those who believed as he, much easier. He smiled and tapped the brim of his hat, nodding,

"Not yet, lads. I'm still looking for her."

The Forgotten Mermaid   by Gregga J. Johnn

One of the more belligerent fire attendees slurred,

"An' wha' maykes you fink you'll even find such a fing?"

Brice smiled and swaggered on,

"Faith, my friend," he sighed quietly to himself, "Faith."

They wouldn't let it go, so one more yelled after him,

"Faith in wha Cap't Delusion? The wind? She's a harsh mistress to follow, always at your back, never at your beckoning."

The Captain stopped to advise his fellow sea-mate,

"Trying to control the wind and keep her at your beck and call will only drive you mad, good sir. It's in letting her fill your sails and take you where she will that gets you into her arms." He bowed slightly and informed them all that, "it's Deluse, Captain Brice Deluse, and I am looking for both a crew and information for my quest should you know any local tales."

"An' if'n someone 'ud wanna tell ya anyfink, where will ya be found?" the youngest of the lot inquired.

Captain Brice smirked and said,

"I'm sure those who are truly interested will be able to find me. They only need follow the wind."

Two

The good Captain found lodging in a meager Bed & Breakfast as opposed to the local tavern. With his credibility shot due to his fantastical questing, he did his best to savor even the smallest shred of sensibility. Thus he submitted himself to a luncheon at a table shared with a traveling preacher and his wife in respectability and gentility, while those more akin to his transportation lifestyle swaggered and swore in the town's local pub.

"Are you a merchant sailor?" the young, rosy cheeked wife inquired of him as he adjusted his coat in sitting.

"By trade, yes ma'am." He settled his Captain's hat on his lap and smoothed back the dark waves of his hair.

"Well, praise the Lord, then!" the preacher exclaimed, "We're looking for a decent merchant vessel to acquire transportation on our mission."

"Where are you headed?" Brice inquired politely, determined to be going in the opposite direction.

The preacher paused a moment with eyes closed and breathed a soft, deep breath. When he re-opened his eyes he smiled and said,

"It would seem we are going wherever you are."

Brice was a little taken aback.

"And where am I going?" he smirked in amusement.

"That I do not know, only that it is wherever we are headed." Replied the preacher casually taking a slurp of soup.

Brice, accustomed to being accused of eccentricity, thought that perhaps he might have met his match.

The preacher's wife smiled and placed a gentle hand upon his forearm,

"Forgive my husband's vague commentary." She politely explained, "we are accustomed to being led only a step at a time."

Brice clued in. He wasn't ignorant of the ways of the church. His own uncle had been a career clergyman. Although his career choice was more for the provision of a comfortable home on the estates of a distinguished family and the freedom to roam within the society of such. This uncle was not intentionally a spiritual man. He only taught the ways of the Bible as one might teach a roomful of snotty boys the modern ways of Shakespeare or Milton.

Thus, Captain Deluse couldn't hide his sarcasm as he inquired,

"So, God just told you to follow me?"

"Not at all, my good friend." The preacher smiled back, teasing, "He just told me to follow Him… on your ship."

The Forgotten Mermaid — by Gregga J. Johnn

A merchant ship can always use the guaranteed pay of good fare so Brice agreed,

"Alright then. My ship leaves at noon with the end of the tide tomorrow. But I'll need payment up front. And, of course, your safe arrival at our destination is pending weather, illness, pirates, and tragedy."

The eyes of the preacher's wife lit up,

"Ohhhh! That sounds thrilling. Would you like some more bread, Captain?" She gestured to cut another slice for him.

"Yes, thank you," Brice accepted and reconsidered all he had previously understood about the clergy based on the weasely nature of his uncle.

Lunch continued quite satisfactorily.

Her meal was almost completed as well.

She sucked out the last tendrils of meat from between the metatarsals of the sailor's feet. He had been quite excellent feasting. Now she truly was tired. Not so much exhausted from her miserable loneliness, as being contented with the weariness that comes in a full belly and a secure hideaway.

Never again would she trust the evil of human men. Never again would she believe they wanted anything more from her than to lock her up as a circus freak, or dissect her as a science project.

But for now, trusting that men make good nourishment for a siren's calling, she would sleep a while, and dream of more songs to sing to bring to her the next meal.

Three

Captain Brice Deluse strolled across the deck of his tiny ship, the *Pursuit*. Well, she wasn't really tiny when compared with a dingy, or a single-man sail boat; but when compared with other merchant ships, and especially the looming threat of pirate ships, tiny indeed, she was.

He loved his little ship as with great effort he was perfectly capable of handling her on his own. Granted, alone was unwise and clumsy, but as he was a singularly independent man that did not like to rely upon others for assistance, the manageability suited him well.

It was early morning on the second day in this port town and hopefully his last. He always found that the worst thing about port towns were the people in them and this town had proven to be the same, but for a random meeting. Brice hoped he would not regret granting passage to the odd missionary preacher and his wife. He also hoped the young sailor who had shown interest in talking to him further about his quest might actually follow the wind and find him here. His hopes and trust in the wind served him well this morning.

A small donkey cart was being driven down to the quiet docks in the misty dawn. Brice considered the packages that caused the cart it's heaviness through his spyglass. He couldn't see what belabored the beast, but recognized the driver sitting atop the cart along with an older woman.

The donkey pulled up alongside Brice's ship and he was hailed by the young sailor who inquired of his findability the day before.

"Ho thar, Cap't Deluse. I hears you is lookin for a crew?"

"I am." The Captain nodded and tipped his hat to the crone beside the boy.

"Wew, me mah n I is wunderin if you might consider a deal wif us?"

"A boy and an old woman?" Brice cleared his throat uncomfortably as the air was still slicing cold. "My ship may be small, but I should consider a slightly more hearty fare of frame than either of you appear to bring."

The old lady stood and precariously stepped backward, down from the cart with a grab on her son's surprisingly sturdy arm. She smiled with a partly toothless grin and hobbled closer to the dock's edge and bowed, admitting,

"I know we don't seem like much, but unfortunately we are more trouble than we seem."

Brice snickered to himself unsure if the woman intended to sell herself so poorly.

"Let me explain a little more if I may?" She bowed again.

Brice was quite amused,

"By all means, do as you will."

The woman hobbled toward the back of the cart and lifted the edge of the heavy blanket that covered their wares. The unconscious faces of two burly men snored heavily in the sudden cold exposure.

"These are me boys, y'see, sir."

"Reeeally?" The Captain loathed the practice of shanghi.

"It's true!" the boy accompanying her sprang down from the cart and implored him.

"Me brothers, ya see, well, they're in a spo' of trouble with the law in this heres town... and they're proud men who'd rahver see 'emselves hung than admit theys were looking too highly at the magistraytes daughters." The boy faulted and looked quite distraught.

The woman took up the plea,

"We all need to disappear, as it were, sir." She gestured to the cart that Brice could now tell held two large men, a couple of bags, and a few barrels to spare. "This is all I have in the whole world and its meager pickins, but if I was t' lose me sons like the magistrate has threatened then, as you can see, I would have but barely a morsel left and little life to go with it."

The Forgotten Mermaid   by Gregga J. Johnn

To put the seal on the deal, she added, "He'll steal me boy here, too, for his house boy and leave me with nuttin."

"Huh." Was all Brice could respond before they were all interrupted by the hearty,

"Ho there!" of the Preacher, as he and his wife carefully descended the steps down to the quay.

"We're here, quite early." He babbled on, "I know you said you leave at noon, but I do like to be well prepared… and I wouldn't want to be absent should you change your mind early."

The missionaries nodded their greetings a little awkwardly as they joined the donkey cart, mother and boy on the dock. There was a minor pause as they all waited in the early sun.

"Well then. All aboard." Said the Captain nodding to the hopeful woman.

He gestured to the healthy missionary couple,

"You wouldn't mind assisting my cook with her packages now would you? All hands on deck on this tiny vessel."

"Righty ho!" exclaimed the preacher and he set his hands to dragging the first of the unconscious bodies up the gangplank with the young boy's help. "How exciting. Adventure be upon us, my dear," he called to his wife.

"Yes, darling, what a blessing to be so abundantly filled with company." Nodding to the older woman, the missionary lady deftly tossed her bag over one shoulder, dragged her trunk behind and then pulled a basket onto her hip, following the awkward parade up the plank to their new home.

Brice laughed at the sight of the young woman's hefting, swung down on one of his ropes to the dock, and helped unhitch the donkey.

"We'll have to leave the cart behind, my lady," he winked at the hobbling woman, "but we can keep your donkey in work and feed while there are so few of us aboard and so full an abundance of provision."

They continued their back and forth plank walk until all packages were aboard and stowed in appropriate shelves and hammocks.

The youngest boy blinked around at the full storeroom below deck, amazed at their good fortune in stumbling upon one so wealthy.

"Blimey... you go' a big stor'ouse down 'ere, sir! An' it's soooo fuwl."

"Never underestimate what you see above water with only your eye's son." The Captain patted the boy's shoulder.

"That's what I always say," agreed the preacher as he wrestled the last barrel into place. "But, I agree with the boy, even with good estimation, you do surprise, sir."

"We shall all get to know each other too well, soon enough." Brice moved to return topside. "No need to interrogate now." He continued partially to himself as the others followed him up. "We've nothing but each other, this small vessel, and the wild seas about us for a while."

Thus, as the sun began to burn off the morning mist and the magistrate blinked himself awake determined to put an end to the lives of the dread ruffians who dared speak to his lady daughters, the *Pursuit* sailed out of the harbor under the keen eye of Captain Deluse, with the aid of an eager, meager, motley crew.

The burly brothers below deck continued their temporary snoring in swinging hammocks… and far away the Siren, also, breathed heavily in her slumber still dreaming of what songs she might sing to call to her the next meal.

Four

The dream was breaking. There was no escaping it.

Feet kicked out against the foaming waves, thrashing in the wake of the great ship. He went under. Eyes wide open in terror as lungs began to throb in desperation. There was nothing but darkness all around, dark silence. The screaming of the storm was silenced and in this tomb of wet he felt his body slowly sinking.

Something was pulling him deeper.

He thrashed again, but another tangle caught both his feet and he descended like a pin drop. The quiet enveloping him like a holy dirge.

Yet there was light and peace.

His lungs no longer craved the air. He breathed as one with the waters and blinked in innocent wonder as the seaweed that entangled his feet rose up and wavered back and forth, all about him. There was something in the weeds!

The boy startled as a pair of eyes blinked out just as innocently as he blinked in. Yet still he breathed and still he was pulled deeper into the darkness, yet there was light all about him. There was light in the seaweed. There was light in her eyes. There was light in her smile as she drew closer and the seaweed smoothed out as tendrils of her hair.

The Forgotten Mermaid   by Gregga J. Johnn

She swam to him and kissed his mouth with breath that pushed all the water out of his nostrils. He snorted and sneezed and shot straight up onto the surface again.

A floating ring was tossed down to him and he instinctually grabbed it and was dragged through the rough waves, water slapping against his face as he coughed up all that had once been in his lungs. He shivered uncontrollably as his body was dragged up the side of the ship. Skin scraped against barnacles and oysters yet the boy cared not for the banging of his body. He was too entranced by the image of her face floating below him, just beneath the water.

She smiled and waved. Her tail keeping her still in the turbulent waves. Then with a pounce over the foam, she arched her body up through the air just enough to reach his eye level, then she sounded in the water and her tail splashed him in a cheeky fare-thee-well. And the mermaid child was gone.

The half drowned boy was pulled onto the ship's deck and into the arms of his hysterically crying mother, but his father looked out to sea as if seeing a distant treasure.

The boy, Brice, coughed and shivered and held the memory of his rescuer close to his heart, forever bound to her.

But she screeched at the memory that haunted her dreams. Her cry echoed off the blue, glowing walls and her tears drenched her face. She would feed again, if only to turn off the nightmares of her past.

Sliding off her rocky shelf, she hit the clear water with a splash and swam her way out of the cave, passed the wreckage that she had gathered for her spoil. Gold, silver, and gems stones glimmered up from already open chests that lay upon the bottom of her watery hideaway. Rare metal machineries rusted beneath her bed, and exotic wooden chests still hid in air tight containers the more delicate of materials that she had once desired to dress herself in as she walked.

She wore such splendor no more. She cast it all off and hid it all away like her memories. There was too much light and brightness in her deep past. It burned her eyes and the more recent turning of her cold, darkened heart would have no more of that.

So she swam over her horde and let the blackness of her tongue trace the glitter of her long, silvery teeth in hunger as she imagined what a feeding frenzy there was yet to be had.

Brice startled awake again in full sweat as if from a nightmare. Yet his memories were all that he treasured anymore.

He splashed about his washtub to wipe off the grime of sleep then staggered up onto deck. The cold wind was harsh, but the brothers were proving to be already tried in seamanship and they held the ship on course.

"Mornin' Cap't" Dereck nodded from behind the wheel.

Daves saluted with a grunt from his seat amidst the ropes as he twisted and wound smaller twines together, casting newer stronger cords with each turn.

They were a week into their journey and still avoiding land. It suited everyone well that way.

The brothers were begrudgingly grateful to have their necks saved via a mother's drugged love. It didn't take too long to convince them that their fortunes could be made with the new Captain if they stayed.

"This," Captain Brice stood in the hold and gestured to the newly woken men with his newly settled crew, "is only part of what I can offer as bounty to all who work on my ship.

The brothers stared with open mouth at all the food, spice, exotic materials, and rare treasures that neatly stocked the store rooms of the ship.

Dereck, the thinker of the two, questioned,

"If you offer such wealth, then why must you accept unconscious trickery in order to acquire a crew?"

"Because this is not the first course of *Pursuit*." The Captain replied and walked closer to a wall of the storehouse that had curtains hanging over it. He pulled the folds aside to reveal a delicately detailed map of the open seas. "This is my true calling."

He pointed to the bottom left corner where a feminine face smiled up at them, surrounded by weedy hair that was supported by a shelled and finned body.

Daves shook his head in wonder,

"So you is looking for mermaids, fer reawl then?"

"Are," corrected Dereck.

"Are lookin," Daves accepted the correction as if it happened all the time, as it did.

"I am indeed." Brice admitted. "I don't shy away from telling people such." He watched the faces of the three brothers, their mother, and the missionary couple. "I believe that if my quest be common knowledge and the news of what I seek be spread across the seas, then perhaps that which I seek might find me after all."

He'd wanted to introduce them all to his quest equally. That way he would know sooner, who he'd need to be on watch for… which of them might try to sway him from his task. His money was on the preacher. But the preacher continued silent awhile. It was his wife who spoke first.

"Elohim has such diverse creativity, more than we can ever possibly imagine. I would love to see what wonders He has yet to show us."

Brice stared at her slightly confused.

The preacher agreed,

"I cannot wait to see what marvels we are yet to see." He smiled and slapped the good Captain on his shoulder. "What we shall see, indeed." He said, somewhat ominously.

Brice stood mouth agape.

"What's the heading then, sir?" Dereck waited orders.

Brice stuttered,

"I just said I was not sailing for trade, but to go find mermaids."

"Yes'sir," agreed Daves, "an' which way was ya want'n us to point the ship fer tha'?"

The youngest boy, Daniel, jumped up with his hand out, "I can man the crows-nest if'n ya like, Cap't?" He waited hopefully for use of the spyglass, which was actually his intent rather than to be of any particular use. He liked the affect the spy glass had on his vision as he gazed through it, at the world around him.

Captain Brice handed the boy his desired treasure and walked rather dumbfounded back up to the deck. When he reached the door to his cabin he paused and turned around, again looking at his sparse and surprisingly eager crew following him.

"So, you're all ok with hunting mermaids, then?"

"Aye, sir," was the unanimous reply as if there were nothing odd about the notion of tracking down fantasy.

Dereck summed their thoughts up,

"It's not like any of us have anything better to do, sir."

"Alright then," Captain Deluse sniffed the salty air, looked about the horizons and said, "Let's follow the wind."

"Aye Cap't" Dereck moved up to the wheel and set the course.

Mother D, the woman who brought most of the crew with her, offered the Captain an apple from her galley hold and whispered with slight eeriness,

"Just hope that the mer you're looking for ain't gone and got herself captivated or worse, turned her song against ye." Then she hobbled below deck again to prepare for dinner.

Brice stepped into his cabin, shut the door tight, and decided to get some sleep. Perhaps he might see her in his dreams again.

Five

The storm was well and truly upon them. Most squalls catch a ship unaware, but the *Pursuit* was not as unprepared as she might seem.

Dereck and Daves dashed about as best as they could with ropes tied about them for safety. Even young Daniel was tied tightly and skittering up and down ropes in a valiant effort to trim the sails.

Brice held the wheel, turning her with the voice of the wind. He had no specific course to follow so he let Calypso be his guide.

The preacher came staggering on the deck praising the name of his savior with as much vigor as a profane sailor curses. He lashed himself to the ship's fencing at the helm as he discussed their course of terror with the Captain.

"Lord have mercy, are we to die in this turbulence?" He spat at the waves that pounced over the deck and slapped him like schoolboy's hazing.

"Not today." Brice grinned. The waters ran through his beard making it glisten in the lightning flashes. "Calypso just be toying with us to see if we're worthy to follow her."

"Calypso?" The preacher stuttered, "Heaven help us! God's eye is heavily upon us. This is no time for mythology." He blinked up into the raging clouds and crossed himself.

"I might say the same to you, preacher man." Brice lashed the wheel and stepped aside to go below deck.

The missionary snapped, following at his heels.

"You can't be serious. It's one thing to have a whimsical outlook on life," he sputtered as a waved caused both men to slip off their footing on the stairs.

The water sought out the insides of the ship.

The preacher continued his sermon,

"But this is insanity!"

Brice stopped dead and stared close into the preacher's eyes with a look of wild, defiant glee,

"All sailors be insane, man of God." He spat the last phrase out as a challenge. "We have salt in our blood, ice in our veins, and the heat of the sun in dead irons under our skin." He laughed and moved to unhitch the donkey. "We be only in sanity while away from our oceans, and that be for us- insane."

The preacher stared wide eyed in horror. He glanced down into the lowest belly of the ship to where he had left his wife manning the pump, expelling the excess water from below deck. He glanced also over to where Mother D huddled keeping the fire in the galley stoked, yet contained.

Then he looked back to the mad Captain just as the man pushed by him coaxing the donkey up the ramp to the deck.

"But if you excuse me now, sir," Brice nodded, "me and me ass is going for a walkies."

The preacher fell to his knees and clung to the post nearest him praying fervently for all their lives.

Brice, however, set the donkey to chains about the central mast that now had the sails all trimmed and neat. He nodded to Dereck and Daves who had no idea what their Captain was doing, but knew enough about seamanship to trust the man who knew his ship better than any others.

Daniel shimmied down to the deck and watched as his brothers helped the Captain yoke up the stubborn beast who was more interested in the smell of carrots about the Captain's pockets than he was in the wind and waves.

When the chain work was comfortably settled about the muscular shoulders of the beast, Captain Deluse staggered in the tossing motion of the ship and passed an orange chunk under the nose of the donkey. The ass stepped forward and strained to reach for the treat. Thus, the donkey worked and the metal at the base of the mast began to groan and click.

The Forgotten Mermaid by Gregga J. Johnn

"Thunk" the mast dropped suddenly.

Daniel screamed in surprise.

Dereck and Daves smiled and pushed their back in to help the donkey.

The loud banging encouraged the preacher below deck to pray himself through his last rites. His missionary wife began to cry in her sweat, and Mother D prepared to meet with peace.

Captain Brice however let the donkey have a taste, then coaxed him around with more promises of sweet veggies.

And the mast dropped again, "thunk, thunk, thunking" with each round until it was a third less the height than it had been.

"That will set the second, deep rudder down far enough" proclaimed Brice and he triumphantly slapped the shoulders of his sturdy crew.

"With that and the flat bottom of this here lady *Pursuit*, we might just be able to ride out the rest of the storm as she blows herself about" Dereck sighed, agreeing with much satisfaction.

"That is my intent," assured the Captain. "I think a hot shot of rum be due, now. Daves," Brice instructed, "I'll have the preacher bring you yours. Keep an eye out for obstacles as the first watch."

"Aye, Cap't" answered Daves.

The Forgotten Mermaid by Gregga J. Johnn

"Dereck and Daniel," instructions continued, "get our good ass here down to stall again, brush him down, and get his hay."

"Aye aye, Capt'," the two followed their orders.

And the *Pursuit* bounced and slammed through the waves for the rest of the night on a steady course that rushed her through the wind.

Beneath the waves on the far side of the wide reaching storm, the siren circled.

Above her, another ship foundered and creaked. Its tiny rudder strained against the pressure of the locked wheel, as the wind and waves pressed in against it. Wooden creaking and groaning cried out against the whistling wind and the two tried to drown each other out.

Siren lips smiled as she broke the rudder's connection to the tiller. She had managed to salvage enough energy in her last feasting to refresh her magic. There was a spark of violet black and the rudder snapped off, hanging impotent.

Her silvery teeth glistened in musical laughter.

Suddenly spinning and swimming with great speed, she maneuvered her underwater way through the rocky outcroppings of the island that lay a couple of miles to the west.

But instead of diving to her hold, she swam to the beach, stepped out onto the sand and, on two feet, ran her wet, naked body up the cliffs to a sheltered hut. There, she tossed a gossamer garment over her soaked form. It clung even more provocatively. The woman then stalked across the windy cliffs to her waiting bonfire.

On board the breaking ship, there was a sudden cry from the poop deck,

"Land ho!"

And the ship turned with the waves and smashed into the hidden reef. When the hull split apart, spewing out all its wares, the crew struck out. They cried for help to the violet flames that flickered ahead of them in the dark.

A figure was standing before the light, singing them to her, and every man, for his own self, set his heart to claim her.

She had them all.

Six

That particular storm lasted several days on the water. But on the island, the wind blew itself out of the sun's way.

The siren spent much of her time hidden from sight, but for the occasional twilight dream-walk that drove the shipwrecked crew mildly insane, and then one by one, she terrorized them with her seductive snatch and grab.

She'd disappeared from view as soon as the first of the wretched sailors hit land. Yet her fire remained, violet, flickering enticement over all who crawled between the rocks onto the sandy shore. They were beaten, bruised, and bloody exhausted. She could have taken them all then. But where was the fun in that?

In the quiet of the post-storm morning, the crew began to waken in the sand. The weakest of the survivors were dragged up to the sheltered hut on the side of the cliff. A real fire was made in the earthen corner and they were left there, shivering in shock, fever, and delirium. The strongest of the survivors, all five of them, set out to discover the secret of the purple flame.

They clambered fairly easily up the rough pathway over the cliff face. It was noted that the way was purposely made in the rock by something none of the craftsmen sailors could recognize, and all dreaded to guess.

They proceeded with greater caution and with each whistle of the wind, none of them was sure if the wind was all that they were hearing.

She crooned to them a little as she watched from behind the walls of the towering waves that careened and crashed over the rocky shore. Her vision was clearest when she looked through a veil of salt. For, although she could at will, suspend her fins and use land legs, yet, her senses were duller within the dry.

In the world of wetness and salt, the siren was near unstoppable. She was the vampire of the waves: designed, built, and evolved as the power behind the ocean.

It was a good thing for man that the mer-folk steered clear of them. For as much power as man had learned to develop on land, so too, the mer-folk had done in the waters, but two times more so. After all, dry land only takes up one third of the whole earth, leaving two thirds ocean.

In the same way, as much as man has accustomed himself, though both practice and invention, to the ways of the waves, so too, the mer accustomed themselves, through magic and intention, to the ways of the land.

Thus, when she was upon land, our siren here could move and sense with freedom, yet her movements were slower and more fluid than they seem speedy and sharp under wave. Also, her hearing was somewhat muted, her vision a blur, and her breathing became belabored after a short while.

However, when she ate... well, that is why she had a secret fortress from which to partake of her tasty meats above the saltiness of the water. There she could eat in peace, savoring every strengthening morsel.

So she watched the five survivors from within her waves as they clambered up the cliff and slowly crept their way with ridiculous caution to her cauldron.

It stood on the cliff top as a lighthouse might, to give warning and welcome. A welcome indeed into the arms of the waiting rocks and the cavernous mouth of a desolate beach; and a welcome, indeed, to their death.

The men circled the stone bowl that sat upon a rocky mound like a headstone atop a grave. It was five feet by five feet wide and looked to have once contained something less fluid than flame, but still fluid in reflection. They tried reading the symbols about its edge, but the weather had long since masked its truth.

She crooned a lullaby at them and they heard her in the flame. She nodded in greeting with the smile of her soft, black lips that she kept closed in a kiss for each of their now fevered hearts. For upon seeing her in the mirror of flame, each man began a journey into madness to claim her for their own.

Again, she had them right where they belonged, in the flickering edges of her whim.

The *Pursuit* continued its raging toss from crest to valley of wave after wave.

The preacher was in delirium and Brice snorted dismissively as the ill man feverishly muttered prayers, and praises, and hymns beneath his subconscious breathing. Yet, the Captain was not without compassion and sought to make comfortable the missionary wife as best as he could. For her sake he offered his own quarters to the couple through the days of the storm.

She accepted for her husband's sake and he was transported by the brothers from the swinging hammock below deck, up to the wooden and feathered bunk of the captain's cabin.

The missionary lady sat by her beloved's side day and night, relieved only when Mother D brought food, allowing her a quick breath on deck to use the open air facilities. Captain Brice gave her privacy as she climbed out to the prow to cast out the previous days nourishment from her system through the rope netting that provided such seating over the ocean.

The *Pursuit* gave homage to the search for love, and so the missionary lady gripped Athena's figurehead with one arm and the netting by her side with the other hand. Her feet swung carelessly as she paused a moment in solitary and bare back-sided contemplation.

She sighed, breathing in the rain that raged about her. When her mother had died in childbirth, her father, a simple fisherman, had taken her on many of his fishing ventures, so the waves were a second home to her. This storm that rushed about her, caused no fear or illness in her heart. Instead, it was invigorating and she smiled, harmonizing a hum with the screeching air about her.

When she clambered back on board to wash up, Brice nodded at her respectfully. She blushed, and Captain Deluse thought the color complimented her eyes.

And the storm raged on.

Dereck and Daves held the ship on her windy course, while Daniel hid away cuddling with the donkey, and Mother D kept everyone's belly satisfied.

The Preacher continued his delirium mumbling as his diligent wife took occasional notes of whatever she could make out that he was saying.

Captain Brice watched in wonder of the strong woman and took to dreaming more of his fantastical quest with curiosity as his mermaid desire begin to take on strangely familiar characteristics.

When the five strongest survivors returned from exploring the cauldron, the festering conspiracy grew in their secret hearts. But their ill companions spoke strange words of a nurse-in-waiting who sang health and healing to them, while kissing their fevered brow with dark and luscious lips.

The last of the five exploring sailors never made it back inside the hut. His mates decided to wait out the dark night and look for him the following morning. There was nothing to be done now. So they slept and dreamed of soft lavender lullabies.

Seven

The survivors in the hut awoke with a start as one of them yelled out in shock. Midday sunbeams pierced their sleepy eyes and the shouting continued. The four who had returned from last night's adventure were grumpy with the rude awakening and muttered curses under their breath. But the ill sailors all began laughing almost manically and would not be ignored. The one closest to the fire was leaping about his other ill mates shouting and pointing at them.

As conscious thought seeped out of sleepy shells, the companions were in wonder of themselves. Those who had been injured with fever or scratch could find no cause for un-wellness upon their person. And the two who had lost limbs, and were near death, found themselves still in deep pain, but their appendages no longer bled because they were in fact partially regrown. This caused great fear in the superstitious and one of the victims looked at his partially intact leg as if he might cut it off again for blaspheming new life.

"Poseidon be praised!" shouted the first waker in glee.

"This be a strange happening." One of the first five was quite dubious.

The seven ill mates who had spent their sleep dreaming delusions of night nurses were transfixed by the health of this magical place. Thoughts of eternal youth fountains and money making tours of such wonders began bubbling up in their greedy souls.

"We must discover the secret of this divine place!" Dr. Scrandon, the first to wake, was ecstatic to be in full health again.

"Wha' maykes you fink its divine?" warned Terrigal. He had already determined to keep last night's violet vision of feminine beauty all to himself.

"How can such healing be anything other than Divine?" Rev. Tungston agreed with his mate Scrandon. The learned gentlemen always stuck together.

Tangtak continued staring, bug eyed, and wailing at his partially regrown leg. He was near mad with the shock and began scrambling away from his appendage as if it were chasing him.

Package grabbed him with both arms, the stub of his once severed wrist, still slowly forming and growing.

"Simmer, Tangtak," he soothed his horrified mate, "It be well wiff us this morning."

Tangtak could only scream and howl as the re-growing wrist, that now restrained him, was so close to his face. Barrel took matters into his own hand and punched the loud mouth so as to silence him into the blackness of knockout.

Barrel never failed in his abilities to accomplish knockout.

In the sudden silence, the shipmates all stared at each other, taking stock of the miracle imparted upon them.

Ferrringdell, the ship's first mate, spoke in response to all their expectations,

"We need to stay in the groups that we were in when we arrived, just for order's sake," he stated.

Digby was indignant,

"We aint on tha ship no more, *sir*," he sarcastically emphasized, "So 'oo put you in charge?"

Terrigal backed up his fellow explorer,

"I fink tha' only maykes sense."

Digby retorted,

"You woold."

Dong clapped his hands to get their attention. He'd also been with the explorer's crew and was eager to set off on his own to find his lavender lady. So, he thought it best to distract the others with the most immediately pressing matter.

He pointed to the empty sleep space.

"Dong uz righ'." Munkary, Terrigal's twin, shuffled his belongings about as if he was determined to do something, "We need ta fynd Mugby."

Package, who had eased his way out from under the unconscious Tangtak, accused,

"He was wiv yoos last. Wha'td ya do wiv 'im?"

"Now isn't the time to be accusing our fellows with unknown mischief, Package." Dr. Scrandon tried to reason, "I think Ferrigdell is on the right track, *NOT*" he rebutted the almost outburst of negativity, "not because he is in charge, but because having order may just keep us all alive longer in this foreign environment."

"Fanks Doc," Terrigal puffed up justified.

"BUT," added the ship's surgeon, "equal share in all things seems only fair as we are all equally shipwrecked here."

Munkary and Terrigal exchanged subconscious support and Terrigal spoke for them both,

"Wha' do ya mean, eekwal shaar?"

"Yeea," Munkary chimed in, "eekwal shaar o' nuffin is stiw nuffin so's I dunno wha' yerz er on 'bou'?"

Tungston, the ship's chaplain agreed with the Doctor,

"Mates, we cannot deny that something miraculous is occurring here." He looked about the crew, "we must also assume that there is opportunity for more wondrous happenings." He paused again, as was his ecumenical habit, "Let us join together in brotherhood and agree that whatever else we find here, is to be equally shared among us all."

Galley coughed on the apple he was eating and Barrel agreed,

"Mates?" He looked around at the disheveled survivors, "we're suddenly all mates because you "gen'lemen" are finally equal to us in having nothing then, is it?"

Dong joined in the disgust, grunting with his open, tongue-less mouth and expressive arm gestures wagging in argument.

Package stood next to Barrel and Dong in unity as Galley, also continuing silent as always, showed his support by offering apples to each of the mates, except the two men of distinguished learning.

Ferringdell spoke again,

"Tha' seems clear to me then?" He began pointing and ordering, "Digby, Barrel, and Galley, you guys go an find more wood for fires and see if there's anythin else we missed on the beach in the wreckage. Package n Dong, you stay 'ere with Tangtak 'ncase he tries to lob off his leg, again… oh, an wait to see if Mugby finds 'is way back 'ere. The twins n I 'll go back to the light bowl an' see if we can find out any more about the weirdness going on 'ere. K?"

Out of habit, everyone just agreed with the first mate.

"Yoo two," Feringdell pointed to the gentlemen, Dr. Scrandon and Rev. Tungston, "We 'r gonna need to eat something when we all get back. Why don' you serve us tonight?"

There was a rousing giggle among all the lesser men, but the gentlemen readily agreed and set about to go fishing.

The Siren licked her lips from her seat where she'd been listening, outside the chimney. She'd been secretly sunning herself on the cliff edge side of the hut. She always like fishing.

Further out over the ocean, morning broke above the *Pursuit* with bright care and everyone found themselves on deck in the sunshine.

Captain Deluse gave aid to the preacher's wife as her weak, young husband was carried out to the deck and walked slowly around upon unsteady legs.

"Does your belly fare better in the sunshine and clear air, my beloved?" His wife inquired.

"Indeed it does, dear heart." The missionary set himself upon a barrel near Daves and requested, "I wish to be useful even in my immobility, Daves, can you share your knotting knowledge with me that I might keep maintenance with you?"

Daves nodded and somewhat silently began instructing the weak fingers in the ways of weaving rope.

"Bailey?" The preacher suddenly called out.

"Who?" Brice looked at him as though he were still delusional.

"My wife, Bailey. Where did she go to?"

Brice stared at him as if he'd heard a magical word for the first time. Then he stuttered,

"Ahh, she... I think she went down to fetch Mema D's breakfast bake for you."

The preacher smiled and breathed with deeper vigor,

"Excellent. This clean, sea air is making me want food again."

The Captain set off a moment then paused and turned back,

"What is your first name?" He asked, baffled with himself that he had gone this far without ever inquiring.

"Barnabus." Said the missionary.

"Barnabus and Bailey." Repeated the Captain.

"Yes. We two are matched well in tongue and temper." sighed the love-struck preacher man.

Brice partially mumbled,

"So, it would seem."

Dereck stood by the steering column and called,

"Where will the wind take us taday, d'ya think, sir?"

"Closer to where she wills, good friend." Brice breathed deeply and moved to stand at the very prow with his back to all behind him… "To where she wills," the Captain repeated to himself.

Eight

Package was suddenly wearier than he thought he should be and laid down on his mat to sleep. Tangtak was still quite unconscious, thanks to Barrel's well aimed punch.

This left Dong to care for the two and keep the fire burning. Dong was not a caring soul by nature, however, and in his thinking, the best thing to do for two sleeping invalids was to let them sleep.

He quietly exited the little cabin and deftly crept along the pathway in the opposite direction than the twins and first mate had taken, some minutes before. Dong believed that to investigate the light bowl was a waste of time. Dong knew what it was that they were looking for and was well versed in the ways of the magical. His mother was a river gypsy and raised him with all the lore and tradition of her people.

Dong knew he would find her in her den. What he didn't realize was that *he* had already been found.

She quickly stepped up behind him, wrapped her arms lovingly about his neck and whispered secrets into his ear. He froze in adoration as she ran a finger across his neck. Her nail glowed a luminescent lavender as it cut like ice, opening his skin, and releasing the surging blood beneath to squirt out. She tossed him off the cliff and dove off to follow him beneath the waves.

The Forgotten Mermaid						by Gregga J. Johnn

On the "*Pursuit*," Captain Brice spent most of his days digging through old parchment rolls and book volumes, writing his own copious notes. He kept his cabin door securely locked at all times and the crew let him be. They were happy to be trusted well enough and simply sailed as they willed. Occasionally they'd stop at a small island port to stretch their land legs and take on more fresh food and water.

Mama D's family stayed closest to the ship and only barely went onto the dock to fetch and load. The young boy, Dan, scampered around on and off the other ships and learned many rumors of how his brothers' escape from hanging had now labeled them as pirates. Mama hobbled around with more bend to her body than necessary. She found the guise of a crippled old crone got her into many places unnoticed. The food and beverage pantry on board benefited from the generosity her appearance granted her.

The missionary couple visited religious sanctuaries in each place and sought healing for the preacher man who continued ill as his sea sickness panned out to be much, much more.

Bailey, his devoted wife, hid her distress well within the strength of her womanhood. Yet, she was not as unaware in preoccupation with her husband's illness as many presumed her to be.

Bailey stood outside the Captain's cabin. Brice had gone into town to seek out the wisdom found in the unsteady mind of a village loon. So, the preacher's wife listened carefully on the quiet ship. She was more and more curious about this unique Captain. There was something strangely different about his person.

Unusual sounds echoed when he was in his cabin, clicking and tapping, and she was sure she'd heard other voices. She strained her ears, leaning up against the door trying to understand the whirring that seemed to hum from within. She wished she'd paid more attention to her brother's lessons in thievery.

Sighing, Bailey set her heart upon pure intentions again. She'd learned by observation, what a life of deception can do. But as she stepped back to move away, she found herself leaning heavily up against the full figure of the sudden returned Captain Deluse. For some reason, she did not move.

His body continued breathing steadily against hers as he asked,

"Is there something I may help you with, my lady?"

She felt strangely at ease with the powerful man.

"There were odd noises coming from your cabin." Bailey quietly leaned a little closer to him, just barely, as if shifting her balance. "I was concerned there was something amiss."

Brice leaned his head down toward her neck and whispered in her ear,

"Things are amiss, my lady. But only because you perceive them to be." He gently placed his hand upon her waist, pressing himself against her more fully as he passed her by in the small hall space. Brazenly leaving his arm around her figure, he unlocked the door before them, pushed it open, and paused to stare deeply into her eyes a moment.

Bailey could barely breathe, her mind raced in a thousand different directions.

The Captain smiled, lifted his hand off her and tapped the outer corner of his eye in a strange salute.

"Good day, m'lady." He said, then he bowed slightly and walked into the depths of his room.

The lady stood immoveable staring after him unable to contend against his gentle confidence. He tossed his hat upon his desk and turned to gaze upon her figure again. Then he smiled, slyly winked at her, and made such a slight gesture with his fingers that she almost didn't catch it. It was as if he beckoned something to pass by his person, but then the door slammed shut of its own will.

Bailey was left without, quite baffled.

Digby, Barrel, and the silent Galley picked their way through the wreckage that continued to wash up onto the shore. They should have realized there was a distinct lack of bloated, dead flesh being washed up also, but they didn't.

Galley and Barrel were the best of mates so naturally there was some eager rough housing between them as they raced each other to pick through the various treasures left on the sands.

Digby made his way along the rocky platform that hugged the cliff face at the beach's end. He found a few nick-knacks here and there among the rocky pools, like the surgeon's bag that was splayed out with various instruments rolling on the tidal rocks. Digby thought he might gain favor with the gentleman if he returned such belongings to him, but then he saw a great prize.

Deep under the waters in one of the hollow column pools, the sailor recognized a shelf of oysters. They sat, sucking water in and out of their semi closed shells, and Digby's curiosity got the better of him. He picked up the scalpel that rolled by on the rocky shelf and reached down nearly a full arm's length to cut away and pull up the top most oyster. He sat there watching his reflection in the water out of the corner of his eye as he shucked open the shell to feast upon the delicacy inside, but stopped short in wonder.

The Forgotten Mermaid   by Gregga J. Johnn

A pearl, the size of his pinky finger's tip, gleamed into his greedy eyes. He reached to pull the pearl out of its holding, when suddenly the oyster slammed shut, cutting off both his fingertips. A violet flash with a violent screech filled his senses in discord with his own cry. The column of water inside the tidal pool burst upwards, encased the man in his distress, and then pulled him down into the hidden depths of the pool.

The tide continued gently rolling the Doctor's scalpel as it lay alone on the bloody, rock shelf top.

"Darling," Barnabus inquired, "you look pale. Are you unwell?"

Bailey smiled weakly and took a deep breath of the clean ocean air. She stood leaning against the ships side looking out to sea. Her husband sat with his back against the central mast, twisting a net together as Daves had taught him.

"I don't know why," continued the preacher man, "but I always feel much more energized when I sit here." He patted the space next to him, "Perhaps you will feel better, too, if you come sit by me?

The dock behind them was a bustle and the brothers carted new barrels of fresh water and oranges below deck. Mama D hobbled aboard and Bailey offered her sudden assistance to distract her thoughts away from their wistful wondering.

"I am more than well, my dear." The wife assured her husband with a mildly strained voice.

Barnabus smiled and settled back into his work satisfied that all was well.

Mama D, however, glanced up into the pretty eyes of the robust woman and questioned her with a furrowed grin. Bailey averted her eyes from the silent inquisition so Mama left well enough alone.

On the beach, Galley wrestled the mighty Barrel. Laughter filled the island coastline and the wind flapped happily through torn sails on castaway rigging.

Barrel growled in aggressive, eager tones as Galley, still not speaking a word, pushed against the man and egged him on.

In his haste to out run the hulking chaser, Galley got his feet caught in a sea-weedy mess of ropes and fell splayed outward upon a mess of wreckage. He paused a moment unsure if he'd hurt himself or not. Barrel came up behind and picked him up off the pile. They both looked down as closer inspection revealed a solid iron pike sticking out of the wood, yet Galley's shirt still looked clean and dry so both laughed in relief and moved away from the hazard.

As the wind whipped up cooler, they began gathering all the driest wood they could find to carry back to the cabin as per their assignment. Heading back up the cliff face, they forgot entirely about Digby.

Outside the cabin, Dr. Scrandon and Rev. Tungston were cleaning and gutting a goodly catch of fish as well as one excellent octopus, whose head was soundly beaten against the rocks before being tossed into a slowly boiling pot.

"Smell's good." Barrel said. Galley nodded in agreement and took to chopping the spring onions that the Doctor had found growing on the cliff top field.

"I'd say it was a good day's work." The Reverend nodded and wiped his scale splattered face. He smiled and continued scraping the skins of the silvery fish.

Dr. Scrandon tossed his hair back and suggested,

"Barrel, would you tell the two sleeping in the cabin that dinner will be ready soon. They'll want to eat to regain their strength."

Barrel turned to head inside but paused a moment, concerned for the obviously shakey hands of his cooking mate.

Galley smiled and shook his head to clear his cloudy mind. He laid the knife down a minute to catch his breath.

Scrandon laid a hand on Galley's shoulder and asked,

"Are you feeling ok?"

Galley nodded and shook off the concern with a smile. He sniffed deeply over the softly boiling octopus and rubbed his belly.

"Yeah," agreed the ship's surgeon, "we'll all feel better with food in our belly."

Barrel opened the hut door and stepped back with a snort and a gasp. There was a foul smell coming from inside.

Rev. Tungston cautiously peeked in, stopped, and cursed,

"God damned! What the…?" his voice trailed off in disbelief.

As the door swung open wider, the four men stared in at the two sailors they had presumed were sleeping. Both men were obviously dead and already infested with a full day's worth of feasting flies. Package lay with his cut off wrist resting gently on his chest. The hand was missing again and his entire torso was covered in the blood of his bleeding out.

Tangtak, also, lay in a pool of blood that leaked, putrid and sticky all over the floor from where his leg seemed to have never grown back after all.

"But," Barrel spoke, "we all saw they had healed?" He turned to the gentlemen for an explanation. "How did we see that they had been healed?"

There was a gasp behind them and the three turned to see horror on Galley's face as he stared down at his shoulder. He blinked up at them as the iron pike sized hole pumped out the last of his blood and he collapsed onto the ground.

"But you missed it?" Barrel ran to hold his mate in his dying gasps. In disbelief, Barrel kept repeating over and over, "You missed it, you missed it. You missed it."

Galley finally died seeing reality in the cuts and bruises and truly disheveled appearances of the three shipwrecked men standing before him.

The Siren watched with an amused grin, from the mirror portal in the boiling water pot. Eyes are easily deceived by illusionary magic.

She blinked her long black lashes and licked the dripping blood off her full black lips. Her belly was rounded as was her larder re-stocked full of several sailors' parts.

Digby sat moaning in a cage cradling his missing fingered hand in horror while our pretty violet Siren munched contentedly upon Dong's liver.

Nine

The Preacher man, Barnabus, had insisted upon returning to his hammock below deck rather than use up the Captain's cabin, and he spent most of his hours there. Bailey assisted him out onto the sunny deck whenever he was able and while sitting by the mast, he always perked up a little. But the exertion of breathing inevitably saw him head back to his hammock once the air turned cool. The violence of his cough caused him to lose most of the contents of his stomach each evening. He was entirely unwell.

Momma D delivered a healthy broth to him and took turns with Bailey in feeding him.

"Do you think its consumption?" Bailey inquired of the older woman.

"It could be, but the cough sounds more like to a prolonged dwelling with smoke than just consumption. Though the first can also cause the latter."

"But, I don't smoke?" wheezed the young missionary.

"And I do," proclaimed Bailey. "But I'm well enough."

"I thought you gave that up, my love?" Barnabus looked a little hurt.

"I did, sweetheart." Bailey leaned in close to kiss his cheek in humility, "and I continue to quit after every pipe I sneak a smoke from."

Barnabus looked confused as he tried to remember all the times his wife's indiscretion may have been hidden from him. Bailey simply smiled in her confession,

"It's easy to do when there's wind about and wine to swig away the taint. Besides, after living with your father, I doubt you'd notice the difference."

Momma D asked with revelation,

"So you father smoked?"

"Like a raging forest fire." Barnabus chuckled. "All my childhood."

"Then 'tis possible you took in the smoke from there." Momma D stood to return the dishes to the galley. "A wee one's lungs finds taking in such things easy. I'm surprised you didn't take up the pipe on your own."

"I swore never to," coughed the preacher, "after seeing what it did to him."

"What about you?" Momma D inquired of Bailey, "You seem to be full of secrets."

Bailey shrugged and defended herself,

"I was raised on a fishing boat with sailors. My smoking, drinking, and speaking habits still reflect that, even when I refrain from doing such in polite society."

Barnabus looked to rebuke her deception, but Bailey fluffed back her hair and insisted,

"Just because I behave differently according to the society I am keeping, does not mean I am deceptive or hypocritical. I am me wherever I am. But, I will maintain polite self-control and honor those around me but not offending them with behaviors they cannot appreciate." She stood a little too defensively, feeling interrogated. "Even if that means smoking and swearing around those who find the absence of such judgmental." Then she flounced out in a rather unnecessary huff.

Barnabus tried to call after her, but his voice was constrained by cough.

"Never you mind your lady, Rev. Barnabus." Momma D consoled the preacher man. "The open ocean brings out the wild in all our blood." She winked at him. "You've a goodly woman there who knows who she is. That's a rarity among people."

Barnabus smiled wistfully,

"It's what I love about her. I need her confidence to help me find myself."

Momma D tapped his head rather sharply with a boney finger,

"Don't you go to relying on no one else for finding you. You is you. You is the one who's got to find you." She tottered away muttering, "That's too much pressure to put on any one." She turned and burst out, "We're all just figuring this mess out, dearie. You gots to do it, too, like everybody else. Quit expecting someone else to do that for you."

Cluttering the dishes in the galley, Momma D whispered to herself,

"No wonder her heart is so quickly taunted by another's comfort and acceptance."

Barnabus lay in his swinging hammock hugging his bible. He prayed that God would be his full strength and that his wife might rest in that also.

Right after scavenger assignments were given to the island survivors, Ferringdell lead the way up the path away from the hut, up toward the light bowl. The twins followed hustling each other in habitual rough housing. The first mate, slapped the two into line as they neared the sacred place.

Terrigal whispered loudly,

"Dj'a fink she lives up 'ere?"

"Hoo?" questioned Ferringdell in feigned innocence.

"Tha' violet laydee." Munkary answered for his brother.

Ferringdell stared accusingly at the two who might possibly think they had a chance to steal his love away from him. He glared at them,

"What violet Lady?"

Terrigal stepped on his brothers foot and answered quickly,

"I dunno?"

The first mate began to circle the two brothers using an authority he was accustomed to on the ship,

"Tell me exattly wat you saw..."

The twins puffed out their chests and remained silent.

"I sed," demanded their accuser, "Wat did yooz see?"

Terrigal crossed his arms and Munkary imitated him. They stared defiantly at the shipwrecked first mate.

"Then, let me tell yoo something." Ferringdell looked mildly crazed with passion as he continued to circle, "I tell yoo wat I saw... I saw a magnificent Lady with the most perfect lavender hint to her skin. A Lady that any man may feel led to worship, but that only *one man* might be worthy of luvin." He came to a standstill with his

The Forgotten Mermaid
by Gregga J. Johnn

back to the bowl and declared, "I am tha' man. An there aint no way eitha of yoo two will eva be good enugh for a divine goddess like tha'."

The firmly crossed arms of each twin slowly unwound to their sides in astonishment as their knees began to bend. Then they threw themselves face first onto the ground wailing in adoration.

Ferringdell watched them and froze as he felt the wind blow upon his back and the hairs on his neck prickled in obeisance to some phenomenon behind him. He turned.

She had risen from out of the bowl and her image, in all its lustfully feminine glory, hovered ghost-like over them. There was a swirling about her and even the trees and grass around them bowed to the adoration of her presence. An unknown loud noise hushed out the world and all other cares, as her face beheld them, now all of them on their knees before her.

She sang,

"Any man may feel led to worship, but only *one man* may be worthy of my love."

Then she looked each man in the face with a taunting smile and asked,

"Which of you will be that man?"

On cue, each of the men pulled out a weapon they had been concealing. Ferringdell had his pistol primed and ready in expectation. Terrigal had a blunt stick he'd found and whittled into a short wooden dagger the night before. Munkary had found one of the ship's hand axes.

The twins fell far too quickly upon their old first mate and in tandem discarded his life as one might cast off an anchor in a deadly storm.

The Lavender Lady laughed in delight. Her black tongue licking sensuously across the sharp lines of silvery teeth. She brought her hovering-self down to the two men and whispered in each of their ears with a flick of her tongue on their necks,

"You know there can only be *One*."

The twins faced off.

Their Lady casually sat herself upon the edge of the stone bowl and caressed her fingers through the water that now filled it. She watched in gruesome delight as the brothers slowly dismembered and punctured each other. There were equally matched and experienced in squabbles. Yet neither of them blinked at the chance to destroy the other. They died in a bloody wrestling bout, as they both bled out.

The Siren surveyed the mess with mild surprise,

"Huh," she contemplated aloud, "That was easy."

Then she twirled her hand and fingers in the air as a spray of water burst up from the bowl, doused all three dead bodies, lifted them and dragged them into the swirling. The bloody soup spun and drained down an invisible hole in the bottom until they were all flushed away.

Walking to the cliff edge, she observed the gentlemen return to the hut with their fishing spoils. Smiling and rubbing her belly happily, she crooned,

"Tomorrow's feast looks like excellent fare." She blew a gentle kiss toward them, "Sleep well, my lovelies."

Then she dissolved into the sacred, stone bowl.

Ten

"Land ho!" called young Dan from his favorite post in the crow's nest.

His brothers, Daves and Dereck craned their necks and shielded their eyes through the early sunrise to try and see more of the island pointed out by the boy.

Bailey scurried to the door of the Captain's cabin to alert him of the news.

"It would seem the wind has brought us in view of an island, sir." Bailey called through the locked door.

There was that odd tapping sound and mumbled voices coming through the closed wood, again. What on earth was the Captain hiding in there? The woman strained to hear and almost lost her balance when the door flew open and Captain Brice came surging out, suddenly stopping short, intimately close to the woman's body again.

There was the familiar awkward pause that seemed to stop time whenever they found themselves so together.

Brice asked quietly,

"Are there any unique aspects to this island?"

"What," was all Bailey could think as she breathed in deeply the scent of his cologne?

"Does this island have any specific markings that might give us a clue as to the nature of the place?" Brice still didn't move. He seemed to enjoy watching the paralyzed flushing of color he brought to the woman's face.

Bailey just mumbled,

"Not that I saw. I mean, I didn't even see it. I just came straight down here to tell you when I heard Dan call out."

The Captain stared at her in mild amusement and whispered,

"Your loyalty to me is endearing." He paused only long enough to shift his focus over her head to look at anything other than her face. "How fares your husband this morning?"

Bailey backed up in the narrow hallway and moved to exit onto the deck,

"He is always much energized while sitting by the mast, sir." And she walked out to meet her man and kiss his cheek in affectionate greeting.

Captain Brice watched from inside the hallway, still hidden by the shadows of the interior, and chuckled,

"Well, he would be *energized* by sitting right there, now wouldn't he."

Then the Captain joined Dereck by the wheel and gave instructions for a careful survey of the outer surf as they sailed around the circumference of the island.

The violet Lady of the island swam out to meet this new ship. She was about to investigate the rudder in her usual destructive habit, but something about the underside of this vessel caught her attention first. It wasn't anything she saw. From the outside, this hull looked like any other, but she felt it, and she shuddered.

She slowed her approach with great respect.

Keeping up with the speed of the *Pursuit* as it cut through the waves, she carefully passed her hand along the wood toward the center bulk.

This ship had a secondary rudder right in the middle. She presumed it to be directly under the mast. It was a smaller upside down "v" that gripped the under-waters and steadied her speed.

Yet the Siren sensed more.

There was an energy about the mast's extended rudder and as she raised her hand to touch the soft insulation about the join in the hull, she pulled from it a translucent blue aura that connected to her hands and caressed her fingers like a long lost pet might lap at its master's hands.

She smiled, and kissed the blueness, drawing the energy form into her mouth as one might suck a noodle from the Asian delicacies of the east. Such raw energy revitalized her forgotten soul. Swimming back up to the surface, she carefully peered through the waves for clearer understanding of who was on board.

There was a child in the crow's nest pretending to be busy, and an old crone sucking on an orange, looking dubiously at the island. A rough deck hand stood at the prow sounding off the depths to his obvious sibling that steered the wheel, and a couple stood together, the woman supporting her man, as they fixed their focus upon the turbulent surf.

None of these were whom she was looking for. They bore not the aura about them of the Energized.

Then he came into view.

The Captain moved to the starboard side of his vessel with telescope in hand, scoping out the natural formations of the land. The siren watched him, knowing that in a few turns of the wave, he would make out her stone call-bowl. But, he paused, and dropped his eye view as if sensing something unknown.

She read his aura and the adrenal glands in her body triggered.

The Captain turned slowly and walked to the port side, his back to the island as he searched the tossing waves beneath him. She couldn't move in time.

The Forgotten Mermaid by Gregga J. Johnn

He saw her.

Their eyes connected in a vague remembrance as her hair floated like loose seaweed about her luminous face. His eyes called to her and the energy of his soul reached out to connect with hers... but she dove into the darker depths and hid from him.

Dan shouted and pointed to a bonfire on the beach. Brice stirred his dreaming soul and kept his hopes quiet.

Taking a closer look at the bonfire through his telescope, Captain Deluse watched with distraction as three men tossed wood upon the fire and danced about the sands in delirium trying to get their attention.

Eleven

Dr. Scrandon and Rev. Tungston lead Barrel inland to the great lake that lay in the island's central valley. When the gentlemen happened upon the excellent fishing spot the day before, they'd hoped it was the fresh water source they'd set out to find. There was a fresh waterfall pummeling down the volcanic mountain into the massive clear waters, but the lake itself, still contained salt. The learned doctor suggested perhaps there was an outlet to the ocean beneath the waters somewhere.

When they saw small spouts of water spray being tossed up into the air by some great creature that rippled large quantities of water at once, they stayed clear of the sands and wandered around the waters cautiously.

Barrel's demeanor was diminished since losing his best mate, Galley. He followed along behind the gentlemen, his massive chest caved in. The Reverend was a little disturbed by the affected emotion the man had for his dead friend, but for gentilities sake, he kept quiet.

Dr. Scrandon was entirely focused upon finding an explanation for the disappearances and illusionary disturbances in which they seemed blindly to continue. For, although upon a thorough physical examination with his fingers, the doctor found a gaping hole in the dead Galley's upper chest, yet still, he had not see it with his eyes until after death had set in. He was entirely confounded and it just would not do for the modern man of science to leave such alone.

They explored their way around the lake with great ease in the delightful sunshine. Were it not for the fact that they had lost nine out of twelve of their party members in the last week, had been violently shipwrecked, and could trust nothing about the appearance of their health... the day's stroll might have been peaceful and refreshing. Yet, as is the case with all hearts, it matters little what brightness of surroundings we find ourselves in when our hearts are as dark as the grave.

On the far shores of the clear lake, there was an orchard with rows of trees heavy laden with a fruit unknown to the men. The bright green skins seemed hard and unripe, yet the darker olive ones that appeared ripe on the outside held thick black insides that the men presumed to be rotten. Barrel cared not though and took a mouthful of the gooey, sticky blackness.

The Reverend scolded him,

"If you care so little about your health that you kill yourself on poisoned or rotten foods, just be sure to bother us not with your moaning when it churns your stomach later."

Barrel paused in his first bite, looked the Doctor right in the eye and spat out the fruits in disgust. The pious man sneered with his, "I told you so" condemnation and walked on.

Barrel then smirked secretly to himself and snagged as many of the round olive fruits about his person as he could carry. He then happily slurped and snacked upon the delicious treats whenever the gentlemen were not looking. Such a refreshment came upon him that he began to hum along with his happy tummy.

Dr. Scrandon pushed on through the orchard like a man possessed. He came out into the prairie flowers with a blind eye to the glory of the natural world about him and pressed on again to another spring waterfall that burst out from beneath a rough rocky platform. He scrambled up the natural outcrop and stood in the wind there breathing deeply.

Below him was a quiet pool that the falling spring waters cascaded into, caught within tall rocky cliffs. The sea waves were kept out of this rock formation that was long and hollow as a corridor. It looked to have no break in its hallway of walls that plummeted some fifty feet to the waters. Yet, these men were not interested in the odd, giant bath. Rather, the men of study paused only briefly. There was too much to confuse and confound already.

They continued passed the spring, over the top of the short grassy edging and peered down to the quiet sands of a separated, private cove on the other side. There was no way down to, or up

The Forgotten Mermaid by Gregga J. Johnn

from the beach here, excepting to climb the sheer rock wall itself. So, the men continued.

To their far right, a forest walled them out, thick and tangled, and dubious sounds of wild animals echoed as they drew nearer. They considered the open a safer place, So returned to the cliff edge. It circled the long, channel below and jutted out into the dangerous ring of rocks like a widow's walk. From the bare watching grounds at the end, Barrel saw it first,

"Sails!" screamed the seaman.

The gentlemen screwed their eyes against the sun and made out also, the soft, wind-filled sails that gently blew along the horizon.

"Quickly," yelled the Doctor, "back to the beach. We must build a great fire to be seen."

And the men all ran back the same way they'd come, around almost three quarters of the island again, desperate to be saved off this hideous shell of a mystery island.

She paced her luminous platform.

The soft blue-glow of slimy cave walls and the plashing rhythm of water sucking and slurping in time with the waves brought gentle comfort to her terrified heart. She carelessly picked up an arm and almost took a bite, but the churning of her insides repelled such and she tossed the arm back into her stockpile of fleshly feasts.

The Forgotten Mermaid by Gregga J. Johnn

Falling to her knees, she began heaving the contents of her stomach over the edge of her peaceful hold. Chunks of freshly devoured sailor floated upon her reflecting pool as she wiped her black lips and shimmering tears sparked the lavender glimmer of her cheeks.

She fell into the waves like a ball, curling up and slowly sinking into the depths of her treasure horde. There on the silent piles of golden coin she rocked herself, gripping her arms about her head as tormented memories flashed insistently as jolts from the past.

In her mind she tried to block the images of that white vessel that caught her in its harpoon thrown nets and dragged her onboard her nightmare. Then her desperate show of strength revealed her legged form and condemned her to night after night of contained rape.

In the moments when she refused to turn from her mermaid form to give access to the hordes of lust, she was caged at the prow of the vile ship and carried about, without food or shelter in her beloved waters that waved beneath her. She was their living carving of luck at their prow.

The waves called to her and stretched their arms up to embrace her as she cried out for their strength, but lost hope defeated her spirit and they stole her pride time and time again. They starved her or they savaged her body. They kept her the play thing of the entire crew until

Calypso herself unleashed a mighty tirade against their sins.

She saved every one of the sailors who tormented her. She swam them each to the shores of her new island that they not perish in the turbulence of waves on rock.

And then she ate every single one of them alive...

But, a deeper memory flashed upon her devastated heart; the boy. His eyes of kindness. His gentle reaching to her even though he was dying. She had saved him, too, long ago as a mer-girl.

It flashed harder and brighter, that memory of sweetness. It seared hotter and hurt deeper than all the others. Recollections of that mermaid from long ago, before the siren haunted the inner waves of her heart.

Captain Deluse dove into the water. A ship's rope was tied around his waist, not to keep him afloat, but to follow his lead. He descended beneath the waves to observe with humanly unnatural clarity. And slowly the *Pursuit* made its way around the island seeking, searching, and hunting for a break in the treacherous ring of rocks that kept them off her shores.

Twelve

The trio around the smoking bonfire took a rest. Barrel had tears of hope in his eyes as they watched the flare burst up from the deck of the small ship and slowly ascend with their spirits into the sky. They had been seen. Now they only need be rescued, *if* the ship could make land without wrecking.

On board, Daves put the flare gun away and returned to the prow of the ship so he could better follow the progress of his underwater Captain who led the way passed all the treacherous rocks from beneath the surface. He tried holding his breath as long as the swimmer, but could not keep up. He was quite amazed at the lung capacity of this great seaman whom he'd come to love with the loyalty of a faithful follower.

Young Dan came down from the crow's nest to watch with his brother. Then he said the oddest thing,

"'e stays down there s' long. Its almos' azzif he forgets to come up fa air."

Daves snorted, scoffing. He ignored the nagging feeling that the boy was onto something. Instead he laughed and instructed the boy,

"Tha Capt'n told me 'e almost drowned as a kid. 'e's been workin on holding 'is breaff for longer 'n longer times since. Tha's all."

Bailey joined them from where she'd been watching, seated on the sails half-way up the mast.

"It is an unnatural long time to be under." She commented just as Brice resurfaced for another breath and dove beneath the waves again. Then she slipped away, presumably to check on her husband below deck.

Bailey had other ideas in mind though. She stepped up to speak with Dereck by the wheel for a moment.

"You seem rather close in thought with your brother." She observed, as the wheel man followed the directions his sibling pointed out. They were following the path of the Captain swimming beneath. Leaning against the Captains coat that hung over the wooden fencing of the wheel lock, she left the statement in the air as a question.

"I've been with 'im since we were inside our mum." He winked at her. "That's a long time to understand someone."

"I guess it is." She inquired with genuine curiosity, "Are there drawbacks to being so close to someone?"

Dereck chuckled,

"Well, we did just fall in love with the same girl and both almost got hanged for it. That wasn't so much fun."

Bailey giggled,

"That would be a bit of a downer." Then she wandered back down below deck.

Once inside the darkened corridor, she closed the hatch so she might be alerted to any one following after her. Then she proceeded down the short hallway toward the Captain's cabin.

On this small boat, the Captain's lodgings were on the same level as the galley and food storage locker, just at opposite ends. A few steps beneath that was the crews open bunk quarters and more storage. There was a locked trapdoor at one end that lead to the lowest level and Bailey had only been down there during the worst of the storming to work the pump that pushed excess waters back out of the hull.

She peaked down to the crew bunks and heard her weary husband snoring uncomfortably through heavy lungs. Her heart ached for his well-being. So she set it even harder toward the task she had in mind.

The rest of the crew, including mama D, were on deck watching for rocks and a way in to the island. There was a loud, long scraping sound beneath her, and Bailey held her breath a moment as the boat shifted, passing a little too close to the rocky outcrop beneath. She didn't have much time, so she hurried to the Captain's door.

Pulling the key ring she'd stolen from his coat pocket, she unlocked his door, entered quickly, and shut it again behind her. Looking about, nothing seemed out of place.

Carefully the woman stepped toward the large desk by the back windows. The sun was let in only a little as the glassy openings were small and high. But enough light shone upon the desk that she could readily read the mapping charts that covered them. Most she recognized... no, all she recognize.

Her heart sank. She was so hoping to find... Bailey didn't know what she wanted to find. But, she just knew that something was not what it should be. Or at least, what it should be according to her perception.

The ship shifted suddenly again to avoid a gentle scraping and Bailey lost her balance. Steadying herself with both hands on the desk top a light suddenly glowed up at her and she gasped, stepping back against the wall cabinet behind her. A mildly hidden panel in the cabinetry pressed open at her weight and the light on the desk disappeared as quickly as it had blinked up at her.

Glancing at the open door, she moved to what was more familiar first as she noticed several small vials that looked like medicine... or in her more pagan understanding... potions.

The Forgotten Mermaid by Gregga J. Johnn

She read the labels on them and discovered they were tonics for healing, only more elaborate and whimsical in their appearance. There was something for pain, and something for anxiety, and something for mind expression (whatever that was), but then she saw one for easier breathing. Instantly Barnabus' belabored lungs came to mind, so she took the bottle to pocket. Behind that was what looked like a small rum bottle with a silver label stating, "Dragon Tears Mineral Water."

Bailey considered taking a swig, but the ship bumped up against another section of island rocks and she was tossed against the desk again. This time, her attentions fully turned to the glowing that arose from the flat surface when her hand landed upon it.

She gingerly stood straight, startled by the glow that disappeared again. She lifted aside a couple of the paper charts and tentatively poked the desktop with a finger. Magic words suddenly glowed up through the translucent wood.

Bailey's biblical learning from her husband had her wary of dark deception, but her curiosity and undeniable trust and affection for her Captain comforted her fears just enough to poke it again. This time, she left her finger upon it long enough to read what the words said.

They were not mystical secrets hidden in the desk. There was no dark magic spells written upon the wood. It was the weather report.

Bailey almost laughed at the mundane words. She laid her whole hand upon the desk and shifted more papers around to get a better view of the circular notations.

The moving words flashed across telling a tale that sounded, (were she to read it out aloud), like the town crier reporting important decrees from the governing officials. In fact, it was a story about a successful military raid on a homestead that was hiding a treasonous family. Another column of words alternated with a picture declaring the birth of some important and rather ugly child.

Then, Bailey saw a small circle within a long rectangle that flashed at her as if inviting her to touch it. So she did.

The circle expanded into a series of other open circles that had symbols in them, many of them letters arranged in some odd alphabet whose order she'd never seen before. So, naturally she touched one of the letters she knew. The letter B. The letter B flashed up inside the top rectangle. Bailey touched the letter A. It appeared next to the B.

"Hmmm," murmured the woman and continued looking for the remaining letters of her name. "Do you not know the order of the alphabet, you silly?" She muttered amused to herself as she wondered why on earth the letter Y might be next to the letter U?

The Forgotten Mermaid   by Gregga J. Johnn

It gave her much satisfaction to see her name written in blue glowing letters upon the Captain's desk. She troubled not her heart as to why she like it so much. But rather cast her eye to the end of the rectangle that her name was written in. There was an odd circle symbol at the end. It seemed to have a straight tail hanging off it. So she touched it and instantly a spinning star swirled upon the whole desktop as if it were looking for something.

Bailey stepped back terrified she'd broken it. The desk when dark again. She reached out to touch once more and saw that just as quickly as the star appeared, it disappeared, and was replaced by a long list of informative words that all had something to do with her name.

Apparently there were many others who shared her name, and some variations of spellings even had mechanical definitions. There was even some record keeping system with her name.

"Interesting," she whispered, but then she had a flashing, brilliant idea.

Bailey repressed the first little circle that brought up all the letters and typed in another name: Captain Brice Deluse. The same star flashed only for a second as if it already knew this name very well... and then Bailey began to read.

She'd only gotten about halfway through when she heard shouting on deck as the ship suddenly veered toward the island. She stood up to glance out the high windows and saw only ocean behind. Listening at the door she could discern that the Captain had found a way in, and that her husband was calling for her.

The desk had turned to normal wood again, so she rushed to answer Barnabus' call. Locking the door behind her, she re-pocketed the keys and pulled out the small "Easy Breath" vial.

At her husband's bedside, she put the open vial to his lips and bid him drink a little. When he swallowed, a sudden cough burst up from his lungs. But then he took in a deep, deep breath and smiled at her like he used to smile at her when he was well.

"My darling, you look so tired?" He took her face into his gentle hands and kissed both eyelids as she closed them.

The missionary wife's heart melted and she fell into his arms as he sat up to hold her with strong comfort against his chest. As her ear pressed against him, she heard no rattling sounds from within, only the strong beats of his dedicated heart.

Bailey cried with relief.

On board, Dereck gripped the wheel tightly as the Captain swam them toward an alarmingly solid looking cliff face. Daves exchanged a worried glance at his brother as he directed him straight at it. Yet, the Captain surfaced again with a smile and assured the man to trust him, then dove beneath the waters again steering the ship right into... and through the cliff face illusion.

The ship settled in the calm waters of a long corridor between tall cliffs. There was a gently flowing waterfall at the far end and the ship was guided quietly and calmly toward it. At its base, the Captain climbed back up onto the deck of the ship and suggested they cast anchor there for the night.

Above them, the three men who had signaled from the fire on the beach around the far end of the island, suddenly appeared. The biggest of them jumped into the cold waters with a massive bombing splash. And while his two companions settled into camp at the top of the cliffs, Barrel clambered on board the *Pursuit* to report the tale of woe, terror, and magical wonders of the island.

The crew listened with growing superstitious fear. But Brice smiled and looked very pleased with himself. He had finally found what he was looking for.

Barnabus, strangely well and in full health again, warned them gravely of dark magic and set himself up to spend the night in prayer against such an onslaught.

Bailey cast accusatory glances at Brice and he wondered what ill will she suddenly held against him.

But then he returned to his cabin.

After closing the hidden medicine cabinet noting what was missing, he sank sadly into his chair, understanding all that had and was about to happen. But it was not until he checked his news report and saw the search history and read what had been read while he was gone, that he began to truly grow concerned.

Thirteen

The Siren rocked herself in the depths of her fortress. Her mind and body were wracked by memories that had sunk to the inky depths of her subconscious, but now floated up like bloated fish, poisoned and left festering, in a rotten and putrid stench, upon the shores.

Stolen from her home and forced into the only slavery a female is ever seen fit for, the scorned girl remembered those dark days in the hull and cages of the white whaling vessel. They had feasted upon her, and then in her revenge she had feasted upon them.

But that was only the beginning of her horrors.

She might have survived as a mermaid had she returned to the sweet, icy depths of her mer-home to recover and find respect in herself again.

But, instead she believed the lies of another sweet young boy who made vows to be her servant. He'd found her in her bitterness and with a smile full of malarkey, he promised to take her home to his family and make her his own. And she believed him as all young lovers do.

So, he took her and they traveled above the lands far away from her ocean fair. He kept her safely in a concealed bath in the back of their wagon. Sometimes there was only enough water in the bottom of the basin to keep her barely alive. Yet, he held promises of grand baths on his home estate and so, for him, she maintained her legs by day. By night she slept in what little slush of water the rain granted.

When they finally arrived at his home, she found that his extensive estate walls contained a grand zoo and a magnificent museum full of creatures strange and new. Her new father-in-law was both owner and ringmaster of a glorious carnival circus.

This was the exciting life that her husband had talked of as they traveled: the parties, the fame, the money! All of it enjoyed by the young couple. He as her keeper. She as his creature on display.

He'd even managed to convince her to keep her dignity uncovered. Although he roped her in magnificent strands of glittering jewels, she was not granted shells to hide her feminine form. For, gentlemen came from all over and paid great treasures to see her beauty behind the glass.

For the truly wealthy, and royalty, she was even given as an offering for the investigation of her full womanly form behind private chamber doors.

The mermaid's husband lost all interest in his creature. He hid his disgust deep in his heart, but when she fell greatly ill, from all the exposure, he cared not to keep her any longer and allowed a bargain to be struck with the prestigious Science Academy who desired to understand more of how such a creature might exist. They had plans for a great many experiments.

The fish woman had plans of her own.

Now, quite accustomed to the passions and weaknesses of men, and well experienced in the means of causing men to succumb to such, the scorned and derided mermaid set her heart to a siren's bitterness.

She planned a farewell party with her husband who was in full agreement and delighted at her ideas.

This husband of hers was a weak man, guided by any who pressed their opinion over his. As such, he was a master of innocent evil and always presented himself as the victim that needed another to lead him.

Many were deceived and believed all manner of lies that he whispered in their ears. For all who offer help and guidance find pride in assisting those found in lesser circumstances. So, this husband always had some great need that could only be attended to by whomever he was speaking with. Thus, all effort in living was eased by arranging for someone else to do all his work for him.

In this habit, her husband was blandly unaware of all that was involved in the party plans that resulted in his drunken stupor being slept off in the coffin-like water bath that was intended to carry her to the Science Academy. She was sure his rude awakening in the after-life might shock his easy going nature. But she doubted he would ever understand what had happened, or why.

For a handful of years, the siren wandered the streets as a woefully forgotten woman. She didn't mind groveling in the mud for food by day. For when she was truly hungry, she simply seduced a young man, or young woman even, and had them lead her to their bathing waters, and there feasted upon their flesh while she washed and revived her hidden magic.

Very soon, she had a vast array of wealth and a loyal entourage who treated her like an immortal goddess. She took a new name to herself and her fame began to spread as rumors in a rain storm.

It is said that other immortal creatures of the night began to seek out her magic and insight at magnificent feasts and decadent carnivals, and the glorious Mathilde was named queen over the Festivities of the Night.

Mathilde forgot all her past happiness and reveled in the guts of her present darkness. She sucked out the blood of all who opposed her, and even some innocents who simply got in the way. But it was not long until the bitterness burned within her belly so deeply that her mind got lost. In trying to remedy the pain, she retreated into her agonies.

The Forgotten Mermaid

by Gregga J. Johnn

At that time, her traveling showcase of bloodlust found its summer ending by the cliffs of Sitio, Portugal. Here, in the ancient traditions of holy worship, Mathilde wandered alone on the cliff tops in search of solace.

Solitude is hard come by when you seek it earnestly. Thus is was that a wizened monk interrupted her contemplations as she stood in the wind overlooking the crashing waves of the ocean.

"What is it you seek, my lady?" the pale and ghostlike figure asked her.

"I know not, anymore," she whispered.

"Then you are lost?" he inquired.

"Most certainly, I am lost. I am lost to everything." She was still, so still she was not even sure her lips moved. But the storm raged about her.

"Then you must go home, my lady," the monk responded.

Mathilde gazed down at the waters and whispered,

"Home?"

"Home, yes." Said the monk, "Home you go, then." He stepped out over the cliff face and remained before her, ethereal and inviting.

The Forgotten Mermaid   by Gregga J. Johnn

She reached out to him, as a lamb trusting her shepherd, stepping out to follow him, and plummeted down the cliff and into the surf below.

A mer-guard awaited her in the tossing waves. They arrested her and took her as ransom, home to the kingdom of her birth.

Mathilde spoke not a bubble to any of her own kind, for her heart was too blackened to be a part of her people any more. This made her trial quick and easy. She was found guilty of blood crimes against the lesser Uplanders and sentenced to banishment above the waves on a lonely, wandering island. There, if she found any redemption in her future years of solitude, she might return home again someday. But only IF she could remedy her blackened heart.

But all Mathilde had found on her lonely island was more flesh to feast upon.

Fourteen

Captain Brice Deluse had hunted the great Mathilde and her island shell for a decade now, and he wasn't about to simply pick up three shipwrecked sailors and take them home to safety. For, truly, after so many years living among the Uplanders he had come to care little for their wellbeing, so primitive were their ways. If it were not for the softness in his heart toward the valiant and loyal missionary's wife then he might have used them all as bait.

But then, Bailey had discovered that her Captain was not as she. Brice didn't know just how much the curious woman had read up on his histories. And even though he knew that news reports were extemporaneous with truth, she might still believe their lies.

He must find a way to talk to her alone. This was more of a problem now since she'd healed her husband who stayed by her side diligently. Brice knew that wouldn't last long though... so he waited.

Bailey waited also. She waited until her husband went to prayer. He had taken to descending into the ships belly in the lowest of holds so as to be alone in his meditations. That night, after dinner, when he went "into his prayer closet" as he called it, Bailey confronted the Captain,

"Why have you kept my husband ill all these weeks?"

"I would have him live." The Captain responded without even looking up from his desk when she quietly stole into his cabin.

"You would have him live, so you keep him ill? That makes no sense." Bailey stayed back by the door. She still did not fully understand or trust that desk.

"When your Bacht, or human, bodies recover from illness, of their own strength, then that strength in health is made even stronger." Brice continued reading.

Bailey had a quick thinking mind and was already looking for oddities in the conversation. So, she jumped on his particular word usage,

"*Your* human bodies? Is your body not human, or Bacht did you say? What is bacht?"

"Bacht is the term we use to describe those who live in the Uplands that are not in unity, or at one with the powers of the universe about us." He explained, still reading.

"And what are you, then?" Bailey held her breath, terrified of what he might answer.

"Trevel." Was the singular reply.

"Trevel, what is that? Is that like a merfolk soldier or something? Are you here to capture one of your own kind that has gone rogue? Is that what all this has been about?"

Brice laughed out loud and stared admiringly at the intelligent young woman.

"Come," he gestured to the couch, "sit with me and tell me how you have such brave spirits within you."

"I'm not brave." Bailey was dead honest, for her heart was trembling greatly in the god-like man's presence.

"But you do not blink when I tell you that I am not of your human race, and you return to speak with me after reading, who knows how much, about me from my very own desktop."

Bailey continued still and guilty by the door.

Brice reached into the hidden cabinet and pulled out the bottle of Dragon Tears mineral water.

"Drink with me." He said.

Bailey shrank up against the door.

"You've seen what my potions did to help your husband," he looked at her somewhat ominously, "for now, at least." He poured two small glasses out, "I don't offer anything that will harm you."

The young woman gained courage from knowing how well she had lived on the Captain's ship thus far. She slowly stepped toward him and took the outstretched drink offering from his hand.

The Forgotten Mermaid by Gregga J. Johnn

He raised his glass to her and then took a tiny sip.

She sniffed it. The liquid was clear and bubbly and had a faint, sweet odor to it. Lifting the glass to her lips she sipped a tiny drop.

"Ahhhh." She involuntarily moaned in relaxation.

Brice smiled and sipped his own drink, again.

"Ahhh, indeed," he said. "The sweetest, most refreshing mineral water in the Uplands, or Underlands for that matter, but that is mere opinion."

"The Underlands?" inquired Bailey. "Are you a demon of hell?"

"Not that far under." Brice winked playfully at her and she continued to relax in his easy presence.

"The Underlands are where we Trevel have banished ourselves to save you human Uplanders from having to consider us your gods."

Bailey looked confused, but there was an urgent knock at the door.

"Enter" ordered the Captain.

Mama D opened the door with wild-eyed worry,

"It's Barnabus, sir. I found him passed out in the hull. He's bleedin, sir.

Bailey was horrified,

"Bleeding? Where is he bleeding?" she said, rushing toward the door.

Mama D stepped aside to let her through and followed,

"He's bleeding from ... everywhere, deary."

Brice followed behind with a heavy, sigh of resignation.

Fifteen

Barnabus, the missionary preacher man, was lying unconscious in a curled up, knees bent, prayer pose. There wasn't a whole lot of blood, but blood was a whole lot of places. He was indeed bleeding from everywhere.

Mama D and her sons were huddled in a corner by the stairs in hallowed reverence. Dereck and Daves had their hats screwed up in their hands in respect. Their eyes were wide with fear of the supernatural.

Bailey rushed to her husband but stopped short on her knees before him, not daring to touch him.

The skin over the entirety of his body glistened. He glimmered with a wet sheen of red sweat. The faint odor of heavy sweetness confirmed it was blood.

Mama D quoted Luke 22:44 from the bible in an ominous whisper,

"And being in an agony he prayed more earnestly: and his sweat was as it were great drops of blood falling down to the ground."

Bailey tentatively touched her husband's forehead and felt the sticky, slimy mess. She grimaced involuntarily. But then she glared in slow recognition at her Captain and accused him,

"What did you do to my husband?"

The Captain considered being glib, but his heart truly held compassion and admiration for the young woman. So, he stepped closer to her to keep the others from hearing their conversation.

He whispered,

"There are reasons I withheld my medicinal potions from your husband. This is one of them."

"Is he dead?" Bailey whispered back in terror.

"No," Brice replied. Then he gently placed his hand upon her head and continued, "not yet, but he will be very soon."

"What is wrong with him?" The girl trembled, vulnerable and breaking.

Brice kneeled to pick up the preacher man. He carried him up the stairs to the deck and set him on the pile of ropes by the main mast.

"Mama D," he called to the solemn procession of followers.

"Yes, Capt'" Mama stepped forward bowing out of continued reverence for whatever divine appointment the preacher man was having in his unconscious prayers.

"We need warm chamomile tea, enough to fill a basin, so we can wash the poor man down and make his last hours a little more comfortable."

The Forgotten Mermaid by Gregga J. Johnn

Brice continued with the gentle directions, "The rest of us need to clean the ship's deck, trim the sails, and burn sage for clarity and preparation." He looked at Daniel, "Boy, fetch some hay and the spare sail that's in the mending. We need to make a bed for the man to see him as comfortable as possible."

Daniel inquired,

"Wha' are we be preparin' for, sir?"

"Death," replied the Captain, "Death will visit us tonight."

Barrel began moaning rather loudly. He had stayed on deck the whole time keeping distant communication visually open with the two sailors still camping at the top of the cliff. But now he knew he was not safe, not safe even here upon this ship.

"She's here too! We're all doomed. We're all gonna die!" He squealed.

Without a second thought Brice walked over and punched an undercut to the jaw of the miserable man. Barrel fell silent with a thud on the boards.

The two learned men, watching from the cliff top, finally found their courage and jumped off the fifty foot plunge, landing loudly in the water beside the ship. Their courage had quickened them to the defense of their last companion, but their haste had forgotten reason. It wasn't until they surface blustering in the deep, freezing water needing to be rescued by those they intended to attack, that they realized their folly.

Captain Brice nodded Derek and Daves to help the men on board but had them restrained as soon as they began flailing around trying to defend their knocked out survivor.

"Would you have me settle your spirits as I did his?" Brice nodded threateningly to the unconscious Barrel.

Dr. Scrandon and Rev. Tungston flinched.

"No, I didn't think so," continued the Captain. "I don't have time to explain anything right now, other than to say, if you want to live, shut up and do as I say."

The learned men sat conspiratorially in the corner with the knocked out Barrel. Daves stood by them to physically encourage their subservience.

Bailey crawled under her husband's body and rocked him with her own quiet prayers,

"Please, Captain," she begged, "Tell me what is wrong with him?"

Everyone looked to the Trevel for explanation.

"He is over-sourced." Said Brice. "The potion given to him to revive his lungs was not meant for as vulnerable a frame as his. There is too much... too *much* inside him right now, so it's oozing out of him... and taking his life energy with it." He left out the human vs Trevel details so as to not confound or terrify those less prepared to hear of such wonders.

But, Bailey followed his full meaning.

"You're blaming me for this?" she cried angrily.

"*I* didn't say who it was who gave it." Brice looked sternly at her to warn her not to give away any further secrets.

But, Bailey was too worked up in sorrow and mourning to heed his concerns.

"What are you doing with such poisons hidden away in your cabin, anyway?"

Brice began losing his own temper to his passions for the desperate woman,

"It's my ship. I keep what I will. However, they were hidden so that something like this would not happen. Perhaps, had there not been snooping, thievery, and mutiny going on while I was out keeping everyone from drowning in a sea of treacherous rocks, not to mention rescuing our new friends here, this would not be the sad result."

A lover's spat seemed about to brew, but then...

A violet flash of blinding light burst up from beneath the waters and crashed through to the open air. Above the prow of the ship in a shimmering globe of soft purple light, the Siren hovered in all her gloriously finned and naked form. She bared her sharp, needles of silvery teeth at them and licked her blackened lips with her dark tongue.

The men did not know whether to fall on their knees in lusty servitude, scream for mercy, or run in terror. They stood still with mouths and eyes held wide to take in all the terrifying beauty that was before them.

Captain Brice's heart melted. There she was, so changed from their first innocent meeting. But he supposed he was much different also.

Mathilde screamed at them with banshee clarity,

"GET. OFF. MY. ISLAND."

Sixteen

The humans on the *Pursuit* cowered with hands over ears, shivering in terror at the wailing of the siren. She continued screaming and flew at them with unearthly transparency, flying through them even as a ghost image.

The crew joined in the wailing.

The sound was so great it roused the dying missionary from his unconscious stupor. Perhaps it was adrenaline, or perhaps it was a last charge of energy from the potions he had consumed, but Barnabus rose up and reached out to touch the violet image that careened around chasing chaos all over the deck.

Captain Deluse also stood still just watching in wonder as the siren swooped about them all.

Mathilde stopped her attack and hovered above the two standing without fear.

"I will eat you alive" she threatened through blackened mouth.

"You cannot," whispered Barnabus, his voice failing in weakness.

"I assure you I can and I WILL!" she screamed at them.

The missionary man flinched slightly, but responded calmly,

"You can do nothing without permission from the Almighty and so I say again, you cannot."

"I do not serve your Bacht god. I am goddess here. This is my island and you will bow to me!" Swiftly, the siren flew into his face terrifyingly, drawing her glow about him.

Bailey's courage bolstered in protective defense. She moved to stand beside her husband and held his hand in defiance against her.

Captain Brice baulked for the first time. He'd not taken his eyes off his prize until this moment, but now he took in the solidarity and unity of the godly couple. He, and the remaining crew just watched with awe as the scene unfolded before them.

"I thought you wanted us to leave your island?" Bailey questioned her with polite disrespect.

The siren hissed at her.

Barnabus reached out to touch her face and saw his hand waver right through her ethereal image. He chuckled,

"See, you're not even real."

"I am real enough." Mathilde had already lost her reasoning to panic attack so rather than keep wisdom in her self-defense, projected image, she left the safety of her waters.

This image she'd projected dissipated as she swam out of her fortified tunnel entrance and pushed her tail fin to jump up, out of the water. With a graceful spin of her body over the boat's side, and an added kick of transformation into to her legged form, the siren landed with agility before them in a crouched pose.

Bailey gasped in horror as the woman dared to stand up and hold her regal self before them unashamedly naked.

The Captain couldn't help but smile.

Bailey caught his appreciation and was strangely aroused to anger because of it.

"Cover yourself, you filthy whore!" Bailey grabbed the partial sail that had been fetched for Barnabus to rest on and threw it at the nude woman.

Mathilde barely batted an eyelid and simply brushed the sail aside with a gush of water that exploded from her hand. The sail flapped backwards and entrapped the missionary wife within its heavy weight. It sent her rolling and wrapped across the deck.

Barnabus jumped to rescue and untangle his wife. The siren laughed.

Brice took off his long coat and moved gently toward the violet and black form that had boarded his ship without permission.

"Mathilde," he said, "You are welcome on my ship." Kneeling before her, he raised up his covering in humble offering.

An old instinct kicked in as Mathilde looked down upon the submission of the Captain. Her heart paused a moment in its mania and she nodded in pride. Brice stood again and carefully wrapped his coat about her form as if it were a robe of mink. She adjusted herself within its folds and resumed her regal pose.

Bailey was extricated and resumed her helpmeet support as her husband returned to test the authority of the Siren.

"On what right do you claim that you are a goddess?" he asked with gentle courage, but then his steps stumbled and Bailey quickly held him steady.

"The Great Mathilde has every right to claim whatever she will, or else eat you, Preacher man." Brice warned, "Watch your tongue."

"This." Mama D suddenly joined in the conversation as her sons gazed on adoringly at the siren. "This is what we have spent these weeks pursuing?" Mama D lost all respect in a creature whose form was so humanly more beautiful than she. The older woman spat, "a naked hussy-fish?"

Mathilde looked the old woman in the eye, opening wide her mouth full of silver-sharp teeth. The banshee siren then rushed up, screaming into the old woman's face, while gripping her head with black talon pointed fingers.

Mama D withered into death at the sound and Mathilde dropped her lifeless body at her son's feet. But they were so entranced with her beauty that they barely noticed the loss.

Dr. Scrandon and Rev. Tungston screamed in horror and grabbed at their knocked out friend who suddenly sat up, awakened by their terror.

Barrel took in the scene before him and bolted straight off the ship and into the waters. But *she* pushed another gush of water from her hand at him and he slipped as he leaped off the deck. His head hit the railing with a blood gushing crack. Then his face slapped the water, adding to the spurting mess as he sank into a feeding frenzy of sharks beneath.

"My Lady, please!" Interrupted the Captain, "You forget who you are."

Bailey and Barnabus baulked in shock at the Captain's gentle coaxing of the terrifying siren.

But, Brice continued,

"Please, remember me." He looked purposely into the depth of her eyes.

She didn't blink,

"I know you." Was all she said, as if killing innocents was a normal past time not interesting enough to be acknowledged in casual conversation.

"You remember me?" Brice was hopeful.

"Why should I forget that which haunts my nightmares?" she snarled at him.

Brice coaxed,

"Mine are dreams full of hope to find you."

"Well," Mathilde sauntered to him with full seduction, "you found me. Now what will you do with me?"

Seventeen

"My Lady, please!" Interrupted the Captain, "You forget who you are."

Bailey and Barnabus baulked in shock at the Captain's gentle coaxing of the terrifying siren. But, Brice continued,

"Please, remember me." He looked purposely into the depth of her eyes.

She didn't blink,

"I know you." Was all she said, as if killing innocents was a casual past time not interesting enough to be acknowledged in casual conversation.

"You remember me?" Brice was hopeful.

"Why should I forget that which haunts my nightmares?" she snarled at him.

Brice coaxed,

"Mine are dreams full of hope to find you."

"Well," Mathilde sauntered to him with full seduction, "you found me. Now what will you do with me?"

The Trevel Captain sighed in his heart to see her flaunt herself so desperately. He was not as the other men on board. His heart was not flailing in the terror or adoration that chained reason to carnal instinct. He simply asked,

"Let them go."

"What," she hesitated? It had been a long time since she'd encountered anyone other than the Bacht.

Brice interceded,

"Let them go from your interfering. They are nothing to you. Let them be, as the miserable chattel that they are."

The siren deflated slightly,

"Who are you?"

In answer to her question, Brice saluted her with his right index finger pointing to the outer corner of his eye.

"No." She said in unbelief, "Prove it."

So he bowed again and backed away a few steps. Then he turned and walked calmly up to his steering column. Reaching around and under the wheel, he flipped a hidden toggle and waited.

The silent crew was awestruck by the interaction and thought they had seen all that was possible to astonish, but then something happened that caused explosions of impossible understanding to take place in each of their minds.

The water around the ship began to glow as if something was rising up from underneath. And, indeed, from the starting point of the central rudder on the underbelly of the *Pursuit* a translucent blue glow began seeping up the sides of the hull.

The crew shrank toward the center of the ship away from the edges, but then jumped as the central mast, too, began to have the same eerie blue glow creep up the pole.

The film continued rising up the ropes and encasing the whole ship in what seemed to be a shell of invisible, yet obviously present, blue energy force. When the whole ship was encased, the humans on board suddenly felt as if they were now captured in a snow globe prison.

Captain Deluse reached for another hidden lever.

Derek wondered why he'd not seen these modifications all this time, but when he looked about to see what else he had missed, he suddenly noticed that the newest passengers were covered in grime and bruises, cuts and abrasions as if they'd been battered about upon rocks in a turbulent sea. But they had not looked so beaten before?

The reverend and his doctor friend also noticed their true appearance with a newly terrified understanding of past events. They realized that their perception had been magically altered and there was nothing they could do, but submit to the superior mind and will power of this magnificent mer-woman in hopes that she could love them? A siren's power cannot be contended by mere man.

But, the missionary couple continued to stand against her, at least, until Barnabus suddenly began bleeding profusely from eyes, ears, nose, mouth and fingernails.

Bailey wailed in horror.

Mathilde said with carelessness,

"You're losing your faith-man, Captain." She was relaxing, and walked about the ship as if she was at home.

Captain Brice shook his head in apology to Bailey as he continued by the wheel,

"I'm sorry, my friend. There's nothing I can do." He shifted the lever forward and the whole ship suddenly tilted downwards and began sinking.

Derek, Daves, and Daniel gasped in terror and ran to the sides of the ship as the water level trickled up the side ominously. Dr. Scrandon and Rev. Tungston joined them and watched in shock. Their human minds were unable to contain any level of fear higher than they already knew, so they just watched, resigned to whatever fate was about to overcome them.

Bailey wailed in mourning as her husband failed in his life. He bled out in her arms, holding onto her and gently caressing her face with his bloodied hand in a last, loving farewell before he expired.

Bailey screamed louder than Mathilde had.

The Siren looked at her with an admiring smile and said,

"You're well on your way to following me with that cry, sweetie. Watch that."

Brice continued at the helm and steered the sinking ship deeper under the waves. The waters rose up and enveloped the capsule of blue energy that held the ship in safety and the humans watched in wonder as they began to sail under the quiet channel they'd harbored in. The frenzied sharks were sated and swam curiously past them. Their bellies were not fully satisfied though, so a couple of them snapped their teeth at the observation deck. The sailors flinched in fright but were safe behind the energy force field.

"Did you need to take anything with you?" Brice asked Mathilde.

"Depends on where you are taking me?" she answered.

But before they could continue their inquiries, Bailey stood, covered in the blood of her dead husband, and stormed toward the Captain. She rushed at him and grasped his neck in her surprisingly strong hands and set on him to squeeze the life from him as her husband's life had been stolen from her.

Brice landed on the deck with a heavy thud under her pounce. But instead of pushing her off, he held her close and consoled her agonies. She screamed accusations and vengeance at him. He held her with tender restraint against her strangling efforts and rocked her gently until her raging soothed some and she melted into desperate tears of grief.

He held her as the ship hovered still in the depths of the rocks about the island.

Bailey opened her eyes a little and saw the tossing of waves above them, the rocks about them, and the calm quiet of the ocean deep.

She whimpered.

Mathilde said, unconcerned,

"I do have a few things I'd like to take with me. I would share some with you in thanks for your advocacy."

"I think we'll just stop here a while." Said Brice as he sat up, cradling the mourning widow.

"Whatever." The siren dismissed herself, "I'll need some hands to carry for me, though," she said, looking at the last five males on board.

"I said." Confirmed the Captain with authority, "We will stop here a while."

Mathilde looked as if to challenge him, but he continued,

"We will give way to Death tonight and let him pass from our presence enough to mourn a space."

The Siren sighed in careless disgust.

But Brice insisted,

"I am not so hardened as to allow Death's presence to go unacknowledged." He picked up the trembling woman in his arms and ordered the men,

"See to the preparations of the bodies."

Then he excused himself back to his cabin with Bailey in his arms.

Eighteen

Bailey lay in the Captain's bunk, fully aware of her surroundings, but too exhausted in her grief to interact, or care. She lay there quietly huddled under his covers, listening to him click and tap away on his desk.

He mumbled to himself a few times and listened to voices that seemed to either relay news messages or sometimes just made jokes. Brice intermittently chuckled to himself randomly and Bailey tried to wrap her head around this new, magical interaction with which he seem so comfortable.

What was he? He said Trevel, but that word held no meaning in her mind. Bailey recalled the few snippets of information she had glanced through on his desk.

There had been accusations of treason against the Powers and he had been called a Bacht enthusiast as well as a mer-ambassador, but the tone of the two titles seemed to be both derisive and glorified. She just couldn't make it out.

Perhaps this was all just a dream. She tried to sleep in order to wake.

The Captain's door burst open and Mathilde bustled in with commanding presence. Bailey feigned sleep.

"Knocking would be polite." Brice muttered, not even looking up at her.

"And not leaving me abandoned with the Bacht would be respectful." She snarled back at him.

"My crew," said the Captain, "have my respect. I expect you, as my guest, to give them the same."

Mathilde scoffed, but then she saw Bailey in his bed and hardened her heart toward him even more.

"Men." She snarled in disgust.

"What?" Brice looked at her with returned contempt.

"You're all the same. Sex. That's your only guiding force."

"Do not presume to judge me based upon your own failings, or history." He demanded, standing to regain his commanding presence.

"Oh!" she laughed, "so you dare to claim that you aren't keeping the chattel on board for your own sexual benefits?"

"I dare to claim that I am Captain of this ship and nothing I do is any of your business." He demanded. "Now if you will excuse me, my Lady, I have more communique's to write in order to ready your return."

He gestured with a show of restrained respect toward the door, "My crew is ready and able to assist you with your departure tomorrow. Tonight, however, I suggest you relax and allow them to mourn."

Mathilde looked out the door in shock,

"Surely you don't mean for me to sleep with the crew?"

"Absolutely not. In fact, if you touch or seduce any of my crew, or other guests, I will personally end your life."

With rising panic, she demanded,

"Where am I to sleep, if not here upon the bed?"

"This is your island, my Lady. I'm sure your home comforts are better than any I could offer. And I would never want to presume to bring any woman into my bed who did not come to it eagerly on her own." He bowed and as she stalked out he offered her a, "Good evening."

Mathilde did the only thing a siren, or banshee woman might do. She screamed and rushed out onto the deck, flew around to try and startle the crew, then burst through the translucent, blue barrier out into the waters and swam back to her fortress.

She sat upon her rock outcropping, pouting and chewing upon another liver. They were her favorite.

When she laid down to rest, she noticed for the first time, just how hard her bedrock was. She pouted some more and dreamed up all sorts of vengeance upon her rescuer, all night long.

Back on board the *Pursuit*, Daniel washed both his mother's and Barnabus' bodies with the bowl of chamomile tea. It soothed him and the taut, cold death-skin that he bathed.

The boy made a fine bed with straw and sail. He'd even brought up the drying lavender from the store room to lay about the death. He said it was to ward off any smell, but he laid it all with such careful design that his brothers encouraged him to consider more decoration. This kept the young boy distracted from the horror of his duties.

At the head and feet of the bodies, and at both sides, he laid large metal bowls and filled them with tied brushes of sage, lighting the ends and blowing out the flame, leaving only the smoldering end burning.

A peace settled on board.

Derek and Daves scrubbed the deck with vigor and insisted the two gentlemen give aid also, in the cleaning. Dr. Scrandon asked to examine the bodies, but was denied any access other than a limited visual exploration. The Reverend busied himself preparing words for a typical burial at sea.

The Forgotten Mermaid
by Gregga J. Johnn

As the setting sunlight gleamed, the waves above dimmed and turned golden. Captain Brice gently rubbed Bailey's neck to waken her. She hadn't slept and pretended to not enjoy his touch as much as she did by faking her rousing. Her arousal was disconcertingly real, though. Especially after hearing Mathilde's twisted interpretation of her presence in the Captain's bed.

She moaned grumpily,

"Do I wake from this nightmare, yet?"

"No," said Brice. "But a nightmare is only the past of the next dream that you make it to be."

"What?" She said, still teary as the soul filled ache of her body burned within.

"Come. It is time to say goodbye."

Brice carried her to his chair by the desk. He had somehow captured the scene of a stunning outdoor beach upon the desktop. Bailey started in wonder as it moved and wavered in the soothing motion of waves upon tropical sand. Some baby turtles were birthing themselves up from their buried nest, and she smiled, unaware of the precious healing that such beauty restored to her soul.

While she was transfixed by the imagery, Brice brushed out her hair and gently sponged down her skin, careful to not expose her most feminine self. He helped her out of her old clothes down to the nightshirt and then carefully re-dressed her in long, fitting pants, a supportive tight vest, and a coat of leathery softness.

When he showed her her reflection in his mirror, she remarked,

"I look beautiful?" as if in shock.

"Of course you do." was all he replied, then led her out to the deck.

The Reverend attempted to take his pose at the head of the body to drone out his memorized reading, but Brice shook his head and informed him,

"I am Captain here. The soul safety and guidance of my crew is under my care." Then he stepped in and led the ceremony.

"By the Powers of this Oneness in which we are unified, we bid you, Mamma D, mother of three, and Barnabus, man of faith: fare thee well.

"May the energy it takes for the sun's illumination to reach across vacuous space and touch our faces with warmth and light: brighten your way to your next living."

Brice instructed his crew, "Now, repeat after me, 'Brighten your way to your next living."

The small gathering repeated with him and Brice continued. The mourners quickly picked up their repetition role.

The Forgotten Mermaid by Gregga J. Johnn

"May the energy that flashes the friction of electrics across the sky, inspiring all to seek clearer ways: clear the path ahead of you now."

"Clear the path ahead of you now." The crew recited.

"May the energy of the air that blusters and blows about us in an effort to pass on life and move freshness across the rotation of the earth: pass you on to where you will dwell eternal."

"Pass you on to where you will dwell eternal."

"May the energy of heat in fire that gives light and warmth and transforms simple raw produce into delicacies that delight and nourish our being: burn you into your newest evolution."

"Burn you into your newest evolution."

"May the energies of water that pound and bubble in a continuously refreshing cycle of life: restore your source to its next wave."

"Restore your source to its next wave."

"May the energy built into the breath of fauna, birthing new life through a dizzying myriad of forms: birth in you a renewing of life that cannot be corrupt, henceforth."

"Birth in you a renewing of life that cannot be corrupt, henceforth."

"May the energy it takes a single flora bud to carefully open up so that it may stretch out and feed and grow and reproduce: bloom within eternal memory the glories of all that you have accomplished."

"Bloom within eternal memory the glories of all that you have accomplished."

"May the energy that contains this earth as foundation and casing for the precious core that boils in a molten mass beneath our feet break open: and let you soul pass over into spirit."

"And let you soul pass over into spirit."

"And, finally, may the energy to pierce, to hold together, and to decorate all areas of our lives with raw, or combined metallic force: hold you forever in our hearts and minds to do justice with your remembrance, for as long as we all shall remain."

"Hold you forever in our hearts and minds to do justice with your remembrance, for as long as we all shall remain."

Bailey repeated the last line, again,

"For as long as we all shall remain."

They all stood silent a moment and felt the energy of the world encompass them.

Then a movement made the humans startle. All but Bailey froze in gasping horror as a dark presence passed through them and gathered up the freshness of Barnabus' and Mama D's frames, and their bodies were carried from out of their midst to leave them forever.

Bailey wept silently and leaned upon the strength of her Captain.

Mama D's sons nodded in wonder and respect, then moved to retreat below deck with their guests following them.

Captain Brice Deluse stood patiently calm with the mourning missionary wife; she leaned upon him in consolation. Together they remained statues in the night until her legs weakened and her Captain carried her to his bunk where she slept soundly and restfully.

Brice continued at his desk and made ready preparations for the following day.

Nineteen

"Derek," The Captain called out to the helmsman, from the communication horn in his cabin, "steer the ship back up to the surface."

Derek heard the order from the amplifying horn on deck. He looked at the other men, terrified and confused. They wondered about the deck, within the globe of bizarre blue energy surrounding this underwater ship. The helmsman staggered over to the wheel and looked confused again.

Dereck had been a sailor for most of his life, but this ship that sailed under the ocean was beyond his wildest imaginings. Yet, with an experienced sailor's eye and observant curiosity, the man reached out to pull gently on the wheel.

Instead of being stable, the wheel-post had now been released by the secret toggle Brice had flipped the day before. The whole steering column now leaned in toward Derek with his pull.

The ships prow tilted upwards.

Derek smiled to himself and slowly steered the energized ship back up to bob on the surface of the calm channel again. He then gave his brother orders to drop anchor and the crew settled more calmly in the familiar atmosphere of open air. For as soon as they'd hit surface, the strange bubble of clear blue that surrounded the ship underwater and kept them breathing, dissipated like raindrops evaporating in the heated haze.

The Captain returned to working at his desk.

Some hours later, Bailey was sweating and twitching in her sleep. She was dreaming and it wasn't pleasant.

In her mind, she was back a few days before, stealing into the Captain's cabin again. But this time, instead of a desk, there was a large stone cauldron in the center of the cabin. It brewed a boiling, swirling storm within.

Bailey floated toward the secret cabinet she had discovered and it opened on its own. Inside, a glowing, glass tube rested diagonally on a stand. The bottom end of the tube narrowed to a sharp point, whereas the other end was straight like a blow pipe. But the middle of the tube was bulbous and contained a thick, staining, red liquid.

Bailey saw her hand reach out and take the tube. The liquid inside was warm and seemed to pulse in her hand. With a swift movement she stabbed her upper arm with the sharp end and the red juiciness inside propelled itself down the needle like point and into her own blood stream.

She screamed. The burning was pulsing through her entire body and her skin began changing. She screamed again.

But this time the scream was real enough to drag her out of subconscious terrors and Bailey woke up soaking wet and shivering.

The first thing she saw was Mathilde hovering in pale translucent form by the water bowl next to her bunk.

"You're nearly there, you know." She whispered hauntingly.

"Piss off," was Bailey's response.

Mathilde laughed and cackled back,

"Even closer than you think."

"Where's Brice?" Bailey spat at her, trying to untangle her legs from the wet sheets. She had soaked the bed clothes through with her night wrestling.

"He's resting." The siren nodded backward. "He has a big day ahead of him."

Brice was sacked out, leaning back in his chair with wide-opened mouth, and heavy breathing. His head twitched as if trying to un-see something.

Bailey moved to rouse him out of the stupor, but he was heavily under. The Bacht woman recognized magical handiwork.

"What have you done to him?" she accused.

"It's just what I do, sweetie." Mathilde hovered with a bored look on her face.

Bailey rushed her and ran right through the projected image that then laughed at her.

Ignoring the wretched ghost, Bailey reached for the basin of water that was now in front of her and tossed the cold contents over Brice's sleeping head.

Mathilde instantly disappeared and Brice woke up choking and sputtering.

"What in the bloody hell!" He yelled.

"Sorry," Bailey apologized. "That wench was messing with our heads."

Brice blinked trying to remember his haunting, then snorted in disdain.

"Hmh."

He began tidying up his desk and himself, muttering,

"I'm not going to be able to take anyone with."

Bailey watched him, remembering her own haunting dreams.

She asked,

"Why would she want to put her blood inside me?"

"What?" Brice paused attentive.

"Mathilde, she was putting images in my head of me stabbing myself with some tube filled with what looked like blood."

Brice froze.

"Why would she want to do that?" Bailey kept asking.

"Where did you stab yourself?" he walked to her side quickly, examining her neck and hands.

"I didn't really. It was just a dream." She reassured him.

"Yes," Brice continued flustering about her body, examining her skin and getting alarmingly personal about it.

Bailey pushed him away.

But he continued urgently,

"Where did you stab yourself in the dream?"

Bailey looked at him with great concern and raised her dream stabbing hand to her dream stabbed arm. She dared not actually look at it.

Brice gently folded up her sleeve to inspect the upper arm. Then he breathed a sigh of relief.

"You're ok. Nothing really happened."

Bailey checked her arm herself and rubbed it, repeating her question,

"Why would she want to put her blood inside me?"

"Likely it's not *her* blood she's trying to infect you with."

"Infect me?" Bailey was now really worried.

There was a bang outside as something heavy was dropped on the deck. Brice moved to the door.

"Look Bailey, there's a whole world out there hidden from you for your protection." He paused, "But don't worry. I'll keep you safe." And he slammed out the door, running up to direct the traffic of trunks being carted onto his ship.

Mathilde was moving in.

Bailey wanted to move out.

The woman stomped sullenly down to her own bunk and angrily began shoving all her belongings into her travel pack. Hastily she snatched all her things together with a few of her husband's belongings and then stormed herself up to the deck making an overt show of fed up frustration.

"What are you doing?" Young Daniel asked when she began tossing her belongings into the ship's lifeboat.

"If she's moving in, I'm getting off." Bailey yelled in a loud, scorn-filled voice.

"Ooohh, I like that tone, honey." Mathilde encouraged, "keep that up."

"You shut it." Brice warned the siren.

"You can't go anywhere without us, dear," Rev. Tungston consoled the lovely woman. "Besides, there's nowhere to go."

Bailey shrugged off his familiarity and stated,

"I have a whole, bloody island to go to."

"That's right." Mathilde crooned quietly under her breath.

Dr. Scrandon appealed to the Captain,

"Talk sense into the girl. She's gone mad."

"She's the only one thinking clearly." Brice directed, "The rest of you go and pack your bags, too."

"What?" the crew cried in unison, dropping all that they were doing. There was a shouting match as everyone disagreed with being left stranded on the horrific island of nightmares.

Brice quieted them all,

"Look, shut up!" He breathed a space to ensure he had everyone's attention.

Mathilde seated herself regally upon one of her trunks and listened with amusement.

Brice explained,

The Forgotten Mermaid by Gregga J. Johnn

"I have been hired by the Lady Mathilde's government to find her and bring her in for review. I will now be taking her back to her home place, thus leaving the island empty. It's quite harmless without her on in. And it should stay put, now. So you will be found soon enough."

The Doctor was always listening for scientific oddities, so he demanded,

"What do you mean, 'the island should stay put'?"

"AArrrrghh!" The Captain lost his patience. "I don't have time to explain the mysteries of energy or the world's that are hidden a blink away from you all."

He threw the last of Bailey's belongings into the life boat and became as threatening as he could, growling,

"I'm the Captain of this ship and when I tell you the journey is no longer safe for you, I will put you off my ship, and you will do as I say."

He yelled,

"And that is FINAL."

Mathilde snickered, proud of her tempestuous stirring.

"See!" Brice pointed right at her mocking pose.

He continued yelling at them,

"I'm yelling at you because *she* is messing with my energy." He just got louder, "If you don't do as I say now, we will all be at each other's throats by sunset."

The crew looked agitated,

"Do you want to die?" screamed their Captain.

The men all scrambled to go and fetch their own belongings. None of them wanted any more of the drama unfolding around them. Things had just escalated beyond weird and they all wanted off the ride.

Bailey began unloading her things off the lifeboat and calmly carried them back toward the hatch.

"Where are you going now?" the exasperated Brice snapped at her.

Bailey calmly turned to face him,

"Obviously you can't handle yourself alone with the wench. You need help, and I am the only one without a dick. Therefore, I am the only one who can help you."

Mathilde laughed raucously,

"You stupid woman. You *are* me!" she mocked again.

Bailey took a deep breath and responded,

"Not yet, I'm not."

The Forgotten Mermaid by Gregga J. Johnn

Brice was flabbergasted, infuriated, and kept silent by the siren.

Mathilde sauntered sensually toward Bailey getting up close to her ears and neck as she circled and whispered,

"But how can you resist the call?" she hissed at her.

Bailey dropped her head and closed her eyes breathing calmly and praying silently in her mind. When she opened her eyes again, she beheld the blood-thirsty, scorned and shattered woman before her with a new perspective.

Reaching out her hand, the missionary gently caressed Mathilde's check and said with deep sincerity,

"I forgive you."

Mathilde hissed and the spell broke on Brice.

He interrupted,

"You can't stay."

"Not if you don't let me, I can't." Bailey looked at him with genuine care.

Brice stuttered,

"But... I... You... Your husband just died and it's my responsibility to keep you safe."

Bailey smiled quietly as the other men began returning to deck with all their possessions in hand. They walked a wide arch around and away from the siren, all too eager to be done with the bitch.

Continuing in her soothing voice, Bailey melted the Captain's heart with her resolution and rational reasoning,

"If you want to keep me safe, then keep me. Don't leave me behind on an island as a single woman with five and a half men."

Daniel took offense,

"A half?"

But, Mathilde was not done with her challenger. The siren coaxed,

"She's right. But, it's not her safety you should be worried about."

Looking off to what had been her home prison for the last decade the forgotten mermaid declared,

"If you leave her alone on that island, she will likely be the only survivor. And she *will* take my place."

Brice sighed.

Bailey looked curiously at Mathilde and corrected her,

"You seem awfully confident of what I will and will not do. Do not presume to know me by your own scorn and bitterness."

The Forgotten Mermaid   by Gregga J. Johnn

Mathilde snapped sullenly at Daves who had strayed closer to her in his effort to pack the life boat.

Davies jumped, and looked to hoist the lifeboat over the edge of the ship by himself.

He urged,

"Are we out o' here, or wha'?" He cleared his throat to try and look commanding, "Sirens and sailors 'av always be'n a bad mix."

Daniel and Derek joined their brother and began pulling the ropes to get their escape over the side of the ship. The gentlemen scholars tossed their belongings in and helped with the hoisting.

Brice let the men be in his bewilderment of what to do with this powerfully, strong human woman. Then he looked at the dangerous siren and sentenced her,

"You will spend the entire journey locked in the lowest hold. There's plenty of energy source down there in the workings. You will be comfortable. But more importantly, it will keep us safe from your illusionary tangling."

Bailey took her cue from the "us" and continued down the hatch to return her belongings. She would claim her place beside the Captain on the ship that had become her home.

Thus with scrambled parting, the five and a half men dropped their life boat into the still waves and began rowing out of the channel current.

Brice smirked almost mischievously and asked the siren,

"You wanna help them onto shore, one last time... *carefully?*" he emphasized.

The siren smirked and dove off, into the waves in front of them. The sailors screamed and clung to the boat edges as they swirled and swirled around in a whirlpool that sucked them down.

The boat spun wildly in an energized blue bubble, underwater beneath the cliffs and into a dark tunnel full of oversized sea creatures. The men stared with wide-eyed horror as their human minds burst in fear of the unknown.

But almost as quickly as they were sucked under, they were then spat out again onto a small strip of sand with nothing but a cliff face at their back and the tumultuous, rocky sea in front. The cliffs were climbable, but only with great effort.

The men stayed where they'd been spat out and flopped onto the sand in exhaustion, blind to the *Pursuit* as Captain Brice Deluse sailed out of the rocks, safely below the waves.

Lady Mathilde regally stalked below the deck, escorted by a newly invigorated Bailey. The two women faced off, each strong in her own power. The siren relying upon her bitter energy; the missionary woman relying upon her divine comfort. Bailey smiled as she locked the jail door and returned topside.

The Forgotten Mermaid   by Gregga J. Johnn

Brice was more encouraged than he liked to admit as Bailey joined him at the helm.

He cheekily grinned and said,

"You ready for this?"

"No" she giggled. "But go ahead anyway."

Brice raised his hands, stepping away from the wheel and Bailey felt a strange sense of great energy build up before him.

He pushed his arms out and the whole ship suddenly sped through what looked like a twisting whirlpool under the oceans. They sailed deeper and deeper, picking up speed as they sank.

Twenty

Bailey and her Captain ate dinner out of wax paper wrappings as they stood at the wheel.

Brice kept steering as he munched on the bread and meat in his hand. He had shown Bailey how to make, what he called "bread rolling," by cutting open a small loaf of old, dry bread, pouring meat dripping in and filling it with thin slices of meat and cheese.

Bailey added some of the onions and wild tomatoes they had gathered from the island before leaving and she was delightfully satisfied with the messy, but convenient treat.

"Of course, if you hadn't used quite so much dripping, it wouldn't be running down your arm right now," Brice teased her.

Bailey giggled and licked up the juicy mess off her wrist,

"Oh, but it's so good!"

Brice watched her too attentively and she noticed, blushed, and they both looked away.

There was a bang beneath them.

"I should check on her." Brice sighed.

"Nope." Bailey wiped off the last of her bread rolling meal from around her messy mouth. She popped the last mouthful in and mumbled through her chewing,

"I don't trust her. I'll go."

Just before Bailey entered the hatch, Brice stated to himself in a voice he knew she could hear,

"I would not likely have survived this, were you not here."

Bailey smiled to herself, then furrowed her brow. The way his attentions toward her caused such feelings inside, had always been disconcerting when she was married. And she was still yet too freshly widowed to like the implications.

The missionary widow made her way down to the hull that was hollow and empty now without the crew they'd left behind.

Passed the galley she moved toward the hatch for the lowest deck and the ships energy workings.

There was a pile of old linen siting on a barrel by the door. Bailey stuffed her ears with the thick, cotton ragging and tied a long, turban-like scarf around her head.

Then she opened the hatch, almost falling back on her rear with the force of power that suddenly burst over her through the opening.

The banshee was screaming.

Bailey retrieved the pewter dishware that had been thrown at the walls.

Refilling the cup from the fresh water barrel outside, Bailey then walked toward the iron cage that held her shipmate.

"You realize," she said too loudly as her ears were covered, "that if you were not such a wench, you could come up on deck and partake in the voyage pleasantries."

"You say that every time you come down here, Bacht, and I still won't believe you." Mathilde seethed in her anger through the iron.

"Ok." Said Bailey. "Your choice."

"I have no choice." Mathilde actually spat in the missionaries face. "I'm the prisoner here!"

The gracious lady wiped the spittle off her cheek with a grimace.

"Well that was disgusting," she said.

"No! What is disgusting is a fellow female keeping me in chains?!" Mathilde backed up and actually ran at the bars like a crazed beast.

Bailey couldn't help being distressed. She asked sincerely,

"Is there anything I can do for you?"

Mathilde imitated Bailey's voice perfectly,

"Piss off."

So Bailey sighed, shut the strangely coated door behind her and carried the dishes to the galley.

The Forgotten Mermaid
by Gregga J. Johnn

In the one day that she had been traveling alone with Brice and the siren, she had seen more strange and inexplicable wonders than all her years at sea as a fisherman's daughter.

Brice explained a few things to her, but mostly she simply watched and waited for Time to unfold her fanciful mysteries through experience.

The coating on the inner, lowest hull was the most curious. Brice had covered the entire lowest level in what looked like a thick paint that dried without becoming hard. It glowed like luminescent plankton, had the appearance of slime, but was dry and strangely impervious.

The Captain had called it HdP,

"It's the substance that has enabled my people to live as we do, here below the oceans." he'd told her.

Bailey didn't understand what he meant when he said it was a water plastic, but she was grateful for the way it contained the magic of the siren below.

She cleaned up the last of the meal mess and returned topside.

Brice nodded through the darkness that held thousands of tiny, twinkling lights.

"A plankton cloud!" the woman was all little girl again with wonder in her face. She loved the sea and all its terrifying beauty.

"I've only seen the blue/green kind." She smiled in delight at Brice, "I didn't know there was a gold kind."

"That's not plankton," Brice winked at her and handed her his telescope.

Bailey took the visual amplifier and carefully made her way up to lean against Aphrodite's figurehead at the prow. Holding on with her legs, she lifted the scope to her eye and gasped!

The darkness opened up before her and she saw through. What looked like a film unfocused the details from her vision, but still glimmered outlines of a great city; lights shone in all the windows and along all the streets. The golden glow twinkled in circular fashion, following a winding road, around and around the city, climbing higher and farther up toward a central tower at the top.

It was as if heaven, as a pearl, had landed deep underwater, within the shell of an earthly cavern. Bailey had never seen anything so beautiful. The tears of her heart moving in wonder, blurred her vision even more.

She blinked and sniffed.

Brice was right behind her.

"Bacht, welcome to the world of the Trevel," he whispered in her ear.

"You live here?" she whispered back as the *Pursuit* continued pummeling through the whirlpool toward this glorious jewel.

"No. I live here." He put his hands on the ship's railing.

Bailey dropped her head and ran her hand affectionately over the smooth wood of the rail.

Brice continued,

"But I am from Torres." He nodded ahead.

"Torres?" she asked, still whispering in reverence. She looked through the scope again, "like Torres Strait?"

Brice pointed above to where the ocean surface would be, "the very same," He said.

Bailey's eyes widened, "We crossed the entire Pacific in a day?"

"No," Brice snickered, "that would be impossible. We were already most of the way under when we left Shell Island."

Then he randomly commented,

"Although, I do believe the Senate is working on plans for a carriage of sorts that runs in the Underwaters for passengers to travel across quickly."

Bailey just blinked at his incomprehensible statement.

"It will be some decades, yet, before we can get that up and running though."

She sighed in bewildered amusement and decided to return the conversation to something more familiar.

"Do you have family in Torres?"

"I do."

"...a wife?" she hesitated.

"No. Not this time, although I've had two afore this."

"What?!" Bailey moved back to stare him down, "you've been married... *twice*?"

"I'm a charming man with an ocean for a mistress." He teased, "Women can't keep their hands off me."

He paused a moment and said quieter,

"Of course I can't find any who will put up with Mistress Calypso, either."

Bailey chuckled despite her traditional beliefs in marriage,

"My mother would curse Calypso every time my father set sail." The she laughed again out loud, "But then she'd pray to her to keep him safe."

"Would you like to visit her?"

"Wha..."

"Or, at least the museum and Oracle dedicated to her legacy?' suggested Brice.

"She... she is... was real?"

"We all are, in some sense or another."

The lights were looming now, and Brice slowed the whirlpool in front of them with his raised hand. The *Pursuit* returned to a regular sail.

Bailey watched with a shiver of sacred silence as slowly the ship pressed in against the blurry curtain. The malleable shield sank inwards slightly before engulfing the whole boat slowly through itself.

The ship half hung in the air on the other side, high above and over the open waters of a bustling sea port. Bailey squealed. Yet the ship held in place and slowly descended directly down like a bucket in a well.

When it reached the level of the open harbor waters, she sailed on through.

Bailey looked all around her.

Above on the cavern ceiling was that same HdP stuff that reflected shimmers of blue sky, clouds and even a singular sun force. There were ships and vehicles all about her, some of which swam in the open sky like the birds.

From this ground level looking up into it, the city itself was massive. The poor woman couldn't take it all in. She hid her face in her hands a moment to get her bearings.

"Take your time," Brice encouraged her and pulled her into his chest in a comforting hug. "We'll stay here on board for as long as you like until you get acclimated."

"But what about Mathilde?" she muffled into his strong, secure chest.

"Let's just worry about you for now, shall we?" he squeezed her gently. "Her appointment isn't for a few day's yet. She can wait."

Bailey lifted her head again to peak out the side of her hugging,

"What am I to do with myself here?"

"There are details that will need to be addressed regarding the allowance of Bacht into our culture. But I have you. And if you let me, I will ensure that you are well."

Breathing deeply, the woman gained courage and stepped back to her visual vantage point at the prow,

"I never knew there was so much Life to be lived."

"It's your life. It's all your life to be lived." He actually kissed the back of her head as he leaned in to her again, "Be sure to Live it all." He whispered

The Forgotten Mermaid — by Gregga J. Johnn

The young woman smiled and leaned back into her friend. He'd always given her comfort.

She would indeed live. Bailey would live her life fully, with every breath drinking in whatever came her way. And in this new life, she'd choose to live hard and live well.

Mathilde sat in the bottom of the ship, dwelling on her bitterness. There were still a few days before she'd have to make account for all her blood thirsty ravaging over the last decade.

She considered her recent interactions. Perhaps the dumb human was onto something. As ridiculous as it was, that Bacht woman was able to withstand all the sirens meddling somehow?

The siren, who had forgotten how to be a light filled mermaid, rolled the small vial of thick, staining blood between her fingers before she hid it back in her bosom. She wouldn't waste the dragon blood on a thing as pitiful as a Bacht. She'd save it for something else, later.

But, maybe Mathilde could do as that Bacht did, and let go of her own bitterness. After all, if a pathetic, powerless Bacht woman can forgive and let go, maybe she could, too. She would not allow that someone so useless could do more than she.

Mathilde allowed herself to recall a memory from her happy childhood for the first time in too long. A smile nestled in the corners of her mouth. The warmth of that smile began spreading through her heart, slowly, but persistently. And she began to remember....

Finis

Review Requested:

If you loved this book, would you please, provide a review at Amazon.com?

As a reader, welcome to my family!

Your input it appreciated, so if you have any concerns regarding this book, please contact me personally at greggajjohnn@gmail.com

If you didn't like this book at all, because stranger things have happened, feel free to find another book to read.

My blessings go with you

Peace and Goodwill be with you!

ABOUT THE AUTHOR

Gregga J. Johnn is a transient writer and performer. She has traveled around Australia performing in schools with poetry and puppets, and has over twenty years of experience on stage and small screens, in Australia and the USA; acting, directing and writing.

Currently, she lives on the spirit-filled, Springhill Farm outside Cedar Rapids, Iowa. There she builds her creative business, "Story-in-the-Wings," writing, performing, creating art, and directing. She is often seen as Artist in Residence at Usher's Ferry Historic Village creating seasonal events and Parlor Theatre presentations.

Gregga's published stories are available through Createspace, Amazon, and Kindle. She specializes in Fantasy/Sci-fi and allegory. Much of her musings and creative enterprises can be viewed through her website;

greggajjohnn.wix.com/writer-performer

Passing on the Story of Life is her greatest passion. She believes everyone has a story to tell and cannot wait to hear yours.

END NOTE

(Rating is the author's suggestion only)

The Trevel Story-verse Books & Timeline:

"Bacht, welcome to the world of the Trevel."

The Forgotten Mermaid, *novella [M15+ rating, for mild horror and sensuality]*

Diamonds, Beetles, and Lucky at War, *booklet [M15+ rating, for bawdy profanity]*

The Last Poinsettia, *booklet [G+ rating, a Family Christmas Tale]*

The Tales of the Trevel, *collection of bawdy short stories [M15+ rating, for bawdy jokes]*

The Chronicles of Trevel; Dragon Tears, *novel [PG-13+ rating, YA+]*

The Chronicles of Trevel; Dragon Sweat, *novel [PG-13+ rating, YA+]* (TBA)

The Chronicles of Trevel; Dragon Blood, *novel [PG-13+ rating, YA+]* (TBA)

More books by Gregga J. Johnn from outside the Trevel Story-verse:

Seven Stories for Seven Sons, *Bedtime stories for Imagineers of all Ages. [Family rating]*

The Magical, Fantastical World of Springhill Farm, *novella [PG-13+ rating, YA+]*

How I Saved Myselves; an expose on the inner healing of a "crazy" mind, *Autobiographical booklet [M15+ Real World Issues]*

Save Our Souls, *a play with a short pre-show play, "Thumbs Up, A.OK" (M15+ rating for real world issues)*

Collecting Thoughts and Dreams, *an anthology of short stories and poems.* (TBA)

Intimate Meditations, *a prayer and meditation devotional* (TBA)

Transforming Weakness into Well Living, *a prayer and meditation devotional* (TBA)

Perception, *an allegorical novel* (TBA)

(Rating is the author's suggestion only)

Check out Gregga's website at:

greggajjohnn.wix.com/writer-performer

All books in print are available through Createspace, Amazon, and Kindle.

For special discounts on bulk purchases, contact Gregga at

greggajjohnn@gmail.com

Made in the USA
Charleston, SC
27 January 2016